To M...
Jo...
3
Thanks ... ...ir
hope it ma...
your formida...
expectations!
All the best

A
BULLET
APIECE

SAINT LOUIS NOIR

JOHN JOSEPH RYAN

Blank Slate Press | St. Louis, MO

Book One of the Saint Louis Noir series
Published in the United States by Blank Slate Press.
Blank Slate Press is an imprint of Amphorae Publishing Group LLC.
4168 Hartford Street, Saint Louis, MO 63116

This is a work of fiction. Any resemblance to actual events or locales or
persons, living or dead, is merely coincidental, and names, characters,
places, and incidents are either the products of the author's imagination
or are used fictitiously.

For information, visit us at www.blankslatepress.com
Interior and cover design by Kristina Blank Makansi
Cover art from Shutterstock

Library of Congress Number: 2015943475
ISBN: 978-1-943075-01-0

In memory of my father,
who helped me see through the grey.

A
BULLET
APIECE

1. A FIRE CLOSE TO HOME

Chief Inspector Bertie Albanese flicked the little gray spider scrambling toward his drink and sent it flying off the desk.

"Bad luck, Bertie."

"Yeah? Why's that?"

I rubbed the back of my neck. "Old wives' tale, I guess. Keep one spider around the house."

"Your office count?"

I smiled. "Sure. I'm here enough."

He called Hi-Lo and dealt the cards. I lit a cigarette in the meantime, and offered him one out of dull habit and easy humor. Bertie doesn't smoke. He's working on being a model policeman, too. Chief inspector. Husband. Father-to-be. If he ever quits drinking, I don't know what we'll have in common. A two of spades and a ten of diamonds came up. I called low.

Bertie was quiet for a time as we played. We know each other too well for such a silence to be comfortable, despite what some people say. I wondered briefly, as I often did, if he still felt he owed me. We'd each taken bullets before, and mine was for him. He joked that he'd make it up some day. I'd say time was running out since we weren't getting any younger. I had a knee that broadcast rain warnings and he had a trick shoulder, but other than that we were fit as Ozark fiddles. Whatever the hell that means.

"So, play it straight, Ed. Got anything of interest?"

I looked through my office windows and sighed before replying. "Nothing that isn't heat related. A delinquent kid suspected of joy riding, sneaking out at night and not coming in till right before dawn. I followed him on foot one night. He ran the whole way, too fast for me to keep up."

Bertie chuckled. "What about your car?"

"Too late to go back for it. Plus, I didn't figure I'd be able to stay out of sight."

"So, then what?"

"The next two nights, nothing. Then on the third night, pay-dirt. I borrowed a bicycle—"

"You? On a bike?" He laughed.

"I haven't forgotten. Hurts your nuts though. I hadn't been on one since I was a kid."

"What, and now your package is an impediment?"

"And how. So, anyway, I borrowed a bike. I waited down the street from the kid's house. He lives in Maplewood, near the city limits. He went out on foot, and I was stumbling around on this five-speed, my camera bouncing around my neck, and even hittin' me in the face at one point. Practically gave me a bloody nose. When he got up to Forest Park, I ditched the bike in some trees and decided I'd be better hoofin' it. He took a trail into the woods right at the Skinker entrance."

"Don't tell me."

"I'm tellin'. As soon as he went in, I knew what was up. I thought about the nasty party pics I'd have to take of the kid with some desperate middle-aged man. I didn't have it in me to snap any pictures."

"What'd you do?"

"I got an eyeful of some guy dropping his pants and the kid going down on his knees and got out of there."

"You tell the mother?"

"Had to. She was the client, right? I told her he snuck off into the woods and gave her the intersection. The look on her face told me she understood the implication, but she couldn't acknowledge it. The next night she followed him. With a bat."

"Shit."

"Yes, sir. She beat the hell out of some fat sap and left him in a coma. She dragged the boy home and then beat him. The neighbors heard the screaming and called the police."

"Bad scene."

"Tell me about it. I still haven't gotten paid."

"You're all heart, Ed."

"I don't get paid to write romance novels with happy endings. Just think if I had given her photographs, hunh?"

"True." He called high and beat me. Again.

Bertie stretched out his legs and said it was time for him to take his leave. He had to drop off some paperwork before his afternoon shift, and I made a half-hearted promise to beat him in a chess game soon. As the door to my office opened, the humidity rushed in, even though my office windows face west and the sun was hovering east of the building. My office is a retail storefront in a light industrial court, not too seedy, definitely not ritzy. On slow days, I bide my time watching men in everything from suits to coveralls, women coming off shift work chatting and smoking in groups, and—of all things—children playing outside the experimental preschool across the road. I've never understood whose bright idea it was to wedge a school between medical-technology and paper-clip factories, but I don't mind. The kids' voices remind me of the sea, rising and falling in waves, sometimes rushing at me, other times fading away to nothing. Maybe it's a strange place for a private detective's office, but hey, the rent's cheap.

Some might think blonde bombshells hustle through my door on a weekly basis, looking for help out of messes good looks and bad luck have gotten them tangled up in. Yeah, right. That only happens in the movies. Most guys in this business would be too busy trying to figure out the buttons on her skirt to do anything like solve a case. Myself included. This work's dull, lonely, and fraught with hazards. If a chance came along to help a woman in distress who wasn't a dumpy housewife chasing her deadbeat husband, or an old woman ducking insurance chiselers, I'd be there with bells on—with plenty of gin back in my apartment. But then I already have that, of course.

I looked at my watch. I scratched something dried and crusty off the face of it: only 11:08 A.M. Too early for a drink, but not another smoke. Besides, it was only my second of the day. Lately, I'd been skipping the morning cigarette because my heart started hammering double-time. I'm not giving it too much thought, though. No need for a doc, really. I have a good family history. Besides, it's 1960. I'm sure in ten years we'll all get new hearts at the A&P.

I smoked three more cigarettes, and thought about re-organizing my closed-case files again. Occasionally, I call former clients as a courtesy check-in. Really, though, I'm fishing for new investigative possibilities. I am not a proud man.

Instead, I turned my focus outside. It was just about time for the preschool's morning pickup. From the vantage point behind my desk, I could see part of the front entrance, and most of the fenced-in yard next to it. Amidst the dingy, concrete-laden industrial buildings, the place was fresh, new. Along either side of the entry, late spring irises stood at attention, saluting the sun and greeting everyone who entered. The Bradford pear trees, leaves plump and full of life, promised to provide respite from the soon-to-come Midwest humidity.

First one sedan showed up, then two wagons, then another sedan, then three wagons in succession. Boom, boom, boom. It's a regular bottleneck four times a day: drop off, pick up; drop off, pick up. I recognized most of the cars by now, including which mother goes with which car and which kid. A few of the moms are hot stuff, and they know it. Today, one car I always watched for hadn't shown yet: a snazzy Cadillac coupe convertible, radio loud enough to fill a concert hall. At last she showed. Late as usual. But a tardy's not what I'd slip her.

First, the sharp and tinny bebop strains slid under the thin glass of my front door, followed by the dim roar of the coupe shifting down. As she pulled up to the school, her brakes eeked out the slightest squeal, and she was out almost before the car rocked to a stop. I caught her long left leg as she slid it from the car, then its shapely twin. As she pushed the door further, and stepped out of the car, she stood and stretched her bare, slender arms down to smooth her skirt. A slight breeze caught her brown hair and swished it across her face. She swiped the strands away, revealing full red lips that caused my own lips to curl up in a smile. As usual, she seemed to look over at my window. I always got the feeling that behind her sunglass-hidden eyes, she was scoping for admirers, which probably didn't include the likes of me. She stood up fully and slammed the car door with force ending in delicacy, like she was checking a violent impulse. She headed toward the pre-school door, hips swaying back and forth like they were propelling themselves against each other, trying to burst free from the taut tweed. At the entrance she shook her head to one side to fluff out her hair and examined the effect in the door's reflective glass. Then, holding onto the door handle, she raised one leg and bent slightly to tighten the strap of her sandals. I pulled out another cigarette.

In a moment she was gone, the dark glass sealing her inside. Watching her day after day, I'd started to get ideas. Maybe she'll stop just looking over and come in. Maybe I'll lock the door and draw the blinds. Maybe she'll sit on top of my desk, hike up her skirt, and tell me how bad she's been. Maybe. I lit my cigarette and was about to tap the first ash when the front door of the preschool burst open. It was the leggy brunette, followed by one of the teachers. Although the brunette's eyes were invisible behind her glasses, her fear was evident. It radiated off her like heat waves. The teacher, close behind, was talking, her face a blend of apology and worry. Within seconds, the brunette brought the Caddy to life. She backed the car up, tires squealing to a halt, then, glaring over at my window, slammed the car into gear and peeled out of sight.

It took me only a second to make my decision. I yanked my feet off my desk and hurried out the door. The teacher was still standing outside, staring through the dust left by the coupe. I hustled across the street.

"Ed Darvis." I pointed back at my sign. "Is everything all right?"

The young woman looked at me blankly. She had a ladybug stenciled in paint on one cheek. Then her mouth opened just slightly and she spoke in a soft voice that

trembled. "Her, her husband picked up their daughter. I …
I thought it was all right."

"What gives—?" I began, then stopped myself. From the
tears welling up on her lids, it looked like the ladybug was
in danger of turning impressionistic any second. "So? Are
they divorced?" Real soft.

"No, they're not. I don't understand."

"Has he picked up the girl before?" I hadn't seen any
unusual cars today.

"Only once. That was last year." A certain reality was
hitting her. The tears began their assault on the ladybug. "I
didn't know. I didn't know!"

I reached out my hand and squeezed her shoulder. As I
did, she turned her eyes up to me.

"It's okay. Now, what is it?"

She wiped her face, smearing any hope of retouching the
ladybug. "She … she just told me. God, she just told me!"

I gripped her shoulder harder. My soft touch was about
to go poof.

"Come on, now," I said, "tell me. I might be able to help."

She stared up the road, momentarily composing herself.
Without looking at me, she mumbled, "She said her
husband died last winter."

The teacher turned and ran back inside. To call the police,
I assumed, and I didn't stand in her way. The cops would
reassure her. I would reassure the brunette. That is, if she
came back. Since I was some kind of witness, I stuck around
for the police—it would give me a way in. Another cigarette later, I watched as the young teacher reemerged, again
tearful. She walked around me, looking up the road. I offered
her half a smile and a full cigarette. She didn't take either.

I live in District 9, and my office is in District 2. Although I'm in good with a handful of veteran cops, I didn't know either of the two young guys they dispatched. They approached us warily, jaws set, one easing his hat down on the high-and-tight haircut. As they approached, Mr. High-and-Tight spoke up, "Did you make the call to us, ma'am?" The other officer drew closer to me, looking from behind his shades, saying nothing.

"Yes, I did. I'm Marni Reyes. I called you. I work here." She recited this information with the certainty of a pre-schooler who had just learned her address and phone number. The dark door of the school opened momentarily. I caught a glimpse of grey hair before it closed.

"Who are you?" Officer High-and-Tight asked, standing by me, just out of arm's reach. One hand rested on his hip, while the other hung near his nightstick. Standard police academy stuff. I was about to get smart and ask why I didn't get a "sir," but he didn't look the type to understand sarcasm.

"Ed Darvis." I reached for my wallet. The young cop's nightstick-hand flinched. I smiled at him, slowly took out my wallet, and produced a business card. He looked at it.

"A private dick, huh?" He seemed to enjoy saying that. His partner was sizing me up now, too. Well, good on you, I thought. Welcome to your first encounter with the grey side of the law.

"An investigator, yes," I said. "My office is right across the street. I was watching before the call was made. This young woman here looked distraught, so I came out to see if I could help."

"You were peeping?" The second cop said. Do they train them with police shows nowadays?

"I was sitting at my desk. If you look over, you'll notice the big window of my office happens to face the school." I added, "Kind of hard to miss."

He didn't like that, and I didn't like him. He was wasting time getting tough with me while this teacher wasn't looking any more reassured for having called the police. I still had my wallet in my hand. I handed her two cards. "Please keep one for yourself, Miss Reyes. And if, uh, what is the mother's name?"

"Jerri Hanady."

"Right. When Mrs. Hanady returns, will you give her the other?" I smiled at her, then I turned to the officers. "I suppose you want to take a statement from us?"

Officer High-and-Tight spoke. "I'd like to interview Miss Reyes here. Officer Hamilton will talk to you."

Hamilton stepped forward, expression impassive with his shades on, and touched my arm. Suave. Non-threatening but meaningful.

"Where are we going?" I asked. He seemed to be aiming me towards the squad car. I'd had about enough. "Listen. Kid. Why don't we sit in my office? I've got two chairs, air conditioning even. Coffee in a thermos."

He regarded me, still keeping his hand on my arm. I tried a grin. What the hell, I have nice teeth.

"All right."

I removed my arm from his loose grip and gestured across the street. He followed me, two paces behind. Department protocol all the way.

2. FAMILY SECRETS

Officer Hamilton let up with the threatening manner in my office. Must have been my soothing décor. Or maybe his repertoire is limited to an early campaign of intimidation, followed by standard questions and a notebook. Without the uniform, he'd have the makings of a cub reporter. He had soft hazel eyes without the sunglasses, too.

I gave him all I knew. His note-taking was assiduous. Maybe he was using independent clauses and everything. When he clicked the top of his pen and put it behind his ear, he flipped back to study what he had written. I smoked through the silence.

"You work for the Police Gazette, too?" I finally asked. He reddened slightly.

"I was in J-School before the academy. I did an internship with the Gazette, and ..." He shrugged a little.

"You were hooked."

"Line and sinker." He brightened, happy to complete the expression. I was reluctantly starting to like him.

"Well, if we're finished, I'd like to see about Miss Reyes."

He was business again. "How well do you know her?"

"Just met her today."

"This is a police matter now. If we need anything further from you, we'll call." He took a card from my desk.

"Sure. I just want to see she's all right."

"Mr. Darvis, let the police handle this. We can do this best without interference from outside agencies."

"And what page of your cadet manual is that on?" I pulled out a cigarette and lit it. When I exhaled he waved a hand in front of his face in an effeminate gesture.

"We'll be in touch later in the investigation, Mr. Darvis." He stood up, pushed his chair in, and put on the soulless sunglasses. I watched him leave without a word and then concentrated on the smoke of my cigarette swirling above my head. Officer High-and-Tight was still outside talking to Miss Reyes. Hell, he was probably asking her out at this point. She was looking shyly away. At the approach of Officer Hamilton, she unfolded her arms and turned her head sideways, as if to hide her tears. The first cop had given her a handkerchief to wipe her face, and she made a gesture to give it back to him. He declined, chest out, all gentleman. This tableau was too pretty for me. I opened my bottom drawer and pulled out the remainder of the scotch.

While I sipped at a mug, the cops sat in their car and compared notes. I could see the engine was running from the exhaust. Marni Reyes had gone back inside, accompanied by a grey-haired woman. I finished the scotch and then watched the squad car pull away. As they backed up, they both looked my way, stone-faced. Maybe I should put out balloons.

I waited a minute and then went out the door. Soon, the afternoon pickup would begin, and cars would start lining up. I had a small window to talk to Miss Reyes. A little Sen Sen might not be a bad idea.

I opened the darkened door to the daycare. Inside it was brighter than I'd imagined. Wide, clean florescent lights hung abundantly from the high ceiling. The walls were all done up in different colors. Immediately in front of me was a cubby with a few little shoes. Next to it, a bulletin board hung with sloppy fingerpaint jobs and smiling suns, blue skies clinging dearly to the top margins of the papers. To my right, a reception desk curved into a yellow wall. A heavy, older woman sat behind it, munching chips and looking at a paperback. The latest Agatha Christie. She looked up.

"Yes?" There was demand in her tone.

"My name is Ed Darvis; my office is across the street." I searched for recognition in her face.

"May I help you?" Same tone. I couldn't tell if it was just me or if I interrupted her book, or both. Maybe it was guilt because she was diving into a big bag of chips.

"I'd like to speak with Marni Reyes. I saw what happened earlier with Mrs., uh, Hanady."

"Just a moment." She lay her book down and wiped her hands on a paper napkin. She picked up the desk phone and pushed a button. "Marni? Yes, there's a man here to see you. A mister... ?" She looked at me again. I made a show of mouthing Ed Darvis. She returned unamused to the mouthpiece. "Ed Darvis. Yes. Yes, that's him. You will? Okay." The receptionist hung up and looked at me incredulously. "Go down this hallway"—she pointed with a finger still greasy from the chips—"and turn into the second room on the right." She over-enunciated, like I was four.

"Thank you." I bowed slightly and flashed her a smile. I could feel her watch me over her book as I walked down the hallway. The second doorframe was plastered with two name placards that bore more smiling suns, bright rainbows, and the names: "Miss Reyes" and "Mrs. Simpkins." I entered.

Marni Reyes was seated at a low table with another

woman whom I made for Mrs. Simpkins. Detective work.

"Mr. Darvis. Come in." Miss Reyes smiled weakly and gestured towards a little chair. There are little chairs and then there are little chairs; this one would make a six-year-old fidgety. Seeing my face, she quickly amended, "Sorry. You can stand if you like." I sat anyway, scrunched down, knees practically touching my collar bones. I noticed she had a freshly painted ladybug on her cheek.

"Miss Reyes, I just wanted to come back to see if everything was okay. I mean, with you, first off."

"I'm okay, I guess. Oh! This is Mrs. Simpkins." We shook hands under hellos. "This is Mr. Ed Darvis. From across the street." She turned back to me. "Well, I'm just concentrating on getting through today. Mary—Mrs. Simpkins—offered to take over the afternoon class, but I think I'd better stay. I don't know what I'd do at home except fret." She chewed tentatively at a peanut butter sandwich. With her eyes drawn down and her body curved into the little chair, she looked too young to be a teacher. I bet she wasn't older than twenty-two.

"That makes sense. Keep with the kids here and all." I scratched the back of my neck. "Listen. I'd like to ask you a few questions. I won't take much of your time."

"Are you involved with the case?" The question was innocent, but her eyes lent it astuteness.

"Only as far as I'm a witness and concerned about what happened. Also, I'll be honest, the police will want to find out two things: first, where the child is, and second, what happened to Mrs. Hanady's husband. After that, they'll consider whether to press charges, who wants to press 'em, and who to press 'em against. They're not paid to unearth a deeper story."

"Are you?"

I smiled. "Generally, yes. People don't act without reasons, even if they're loaded with emotions."

She looked at me expectantly.

"Mrs. Hanady was clearly upset. You said her husband had died, yet apparently, he picked up their daughter. That doesn't figure, obviously. The most important thing is to make sure the child is safe. If Mrs. Hanady is telling the truth about her husband, then we might be dealing with an abduction by an impostor."

"You don't think she's telling the truth?" Miss Reyes teared up again.

"I can't say. I need to talk with her myself. If she's telling the truth as far as she knows, her husband may still be alive. Even then it might not have been him who picked up the kid. Then again, if it was him, why did he fake his death? Why did he decide to appear now to get his daughter? If he's alive and it's his child, too, did he break any law? That's a grey area. I also have a friend on the force who can check out Mr. Hanady." I paused. Although I didn't look directly at her, I knew Mrs. Simpkins was appraising me.

"Look, I see I'm upsetting you. I just have a few questions and then I'll go."

Mrs. Simpkins patted Miss Reyes' hand. Miss Reyes sniffled and then smiled, her lips trembling. She didn't break, though, and said, "Okay."

"Thank you, Miss Reyes, may I call you Marni?" When she nodded I said, "First question: Did you see Mr. Hanady pick up his daughter today? And what's her name, by the way?"

"Rachel. Yes, I saw him pick her up. We hold the children in the classroom. The parents come to the door to get them."

"When did you say was the last time you saw him?"

"Last fall."

"And you're sure this is the same man?"

She grinned despite herself. "I'm sure. He's—"She glanced at Mrs. Simpkins. "He's quite good looking."

"I see. What kind of car does he drive?"

"A Jaguar. I wouldn't forget that. Sort of a silvery green. Two-door, V-8."

Interesting. Both parents drive two-seaters. That doesn't exactly add up to pleasant family drives in the country.

"You know your cars," I said, wanting to keep her at ease.

"My brothers and I used to work on them. That is, I used to help them."

"So, did you see the car today?"

"No. Since the parents come to the room, I generally don't."

"Have you ever seen the Hanadys together?"

"No, not in person. Oh! But I do have a photograph. All of the children brought them in at the start of the year." She sprang up and went to a bulletin board. When she returned, she handed me the photo.

It was an outside shot. Nice estate in the background, full summer, flowers, different shades of grey in the foreground. That was Mrs. Hanady all right, this time without sunglasses. Her eyes were greyish, mirth in the crinkles around their edges. I bet they were baby blue in real life. She stood with her arm around a tall man with dark features and a toothy grin—toothy in a capped and pretty way. He wore a coat and tie, and a porkpie hat cocked back on his head. Marni was right; the guy was handsome. Together the couple looked like The First Family. What surprised me, though, was the young girl who stood between them. She wore a floral dress and a big grin devoid of two front teeth. Her skin was tanned dark, darker than the father. Her hair was held back with barrettes. And her dark eyes were barely visible through the squinting folds of flesh. If she wasn't Central or South American, then I'm not a detective.

"This is Rachel?"

"Yes. She's adopted."

"I can see that. How old was she when she was adopted?"

"Two. The Hanadys adopted her from Colombia. They had to go at night, with an armed guard and everything. Apparently, there's some unrest."

"How old is she now?"

"She's five."

"How has she adjusted?"

"Pretty well, I think. She's well-behaved in class and shares with the other kids. She doesn't speak much, but when she does she's very articulate." Mrs. Simpkins nodded over half an apple.

"Any Spanish left?"

"No."

"And the parents? Are they fluent?"

"I don't know. I think Mr. Hanady is. He has investments in Colombia."

"Do you know what kind?"

"I'm afraid not." She glanced up at the wall clock. "Um, Mr. Darvis, the afternoon children will be here soon and we must get ready." Marni smoothed her skirt, which had ridden above the knees.

"Of course. And I've already taken more time than I promised. Miss Reyes, I'd like to help get to the bottom of this. When you see Mrs. Hanady again, will you be sure to give her my card?"

"Yes, I will."

"Thank you. I'll be in touch." I shook her hand, and then the limp hand of Mrs. Simpkins.

As I opened the door to leave, I almost smacked into

the receptionist, who hovered just outside the door. She grimaced and walked towards her desk. I tipped an imaginary hat at her and grinned as I left.

3. CHERCHEZ LA FEMME

Back in my office I put in a call to Bertie. He wasn't in, but I got a half-hearted promise from the desk sergeant to have him call me. If I hustled to the park, I might see him there at the end of his lunch.

I got the Chevy going and pulled out of the industrial court. Heading towards Forest Park, I turned over some ideas about this case. My bet was Mr. Hanady was alive and had picked up the daughter. Mrs. Hanady may have covered and said he died, but that was far-fetched. Wouldn't Rachel have spoken up about it? My guess was they were separated and, to spare embarrassment, Mrs. Hanady had popped out with a lame story. None of that meant Rachel was okay. That kind of upset on a mother's face is hard to manufacture.

Turning onto Skinker, I thought about Mr. Hanady. Smiling, successful. Business interests in Colombia. Bet there's some shady doings on his end, or the wife's. Or both. I intended to find out. I didn't have anything better to do.

I parked near the tennis courts and walked towards the chess tables. A small fountain splashed with the tiny ·rgency of a child in a wading pool. Two old men were ·dled over a table, eyeglasses thick as the German gut- ·opping out of their mouths. A mother and her son walked around the fountain. No sign of Bertie. I sat on a bench to wait.

"You know I could bring you in on vagrancy." I turned around to the voice behind me, and there he was.

I relaxed. "Can't say I'd blame you."

"What's new, Detective?" he asked. He set a foot on the bench and leaned his forearm on his knee.

"I'm late for a chess date."

"We don't have one today. What is it? A girl?"

"You know me. Always on the make."

"Have you made it with a queen yet?"

"Nope. But I met a gorgeous girl today. You'd like her."

"You're not trying to pawn her off on me, are you?"

"Nix. She won't stand before the bishop with just anyone."

"Ah. And you're her new knight?"

"Yep. Wait'll she sees my sword." I paused. "Seriously, I'm glad I found you. I need some information."

"What's up?"

I related the morning incident to him. His casual posture left him. He took his leg off the park bench, and his face hardened.

"Listen. Let me see what I can find out about Mr. Hanady. Got a first name?"

"No. He shouldn't be hard to find, though. Start with the daughter's or wife's names maybe. There ought to be adoption records, right?"

"Sure. I can also call the preschool."

"No wonder you're chief inspector."

"That's me." He stood up, straightening his grey pants, his gold wedding band flashing momentarily. "Look. Ed, don't make any moves until I get back to you, okay?"

I made an innocent face and raised my hands, palms up, as if to disavow any history of trouble with one shrug.

"Where're you going to be later?" he asked.

"In my office. You know, always sort of on the job."

"I'll call you there later."

We shook hands. Bertie departed with a confident stride. He's tall, slender, but his shoulders are powerful. Been married three years to an absolute doll. They're gonna make a beautiful baby some day.

I stopped off for a hamburger and coffee at the Eat-Rite before returning to my office. A little sleepy, I pulled into the court and brought the car to rest in my reserved spot. I leaned over the wheel and looked through the windshield. The sky had gotten overcast. By the end of the day it would probably storm, turn sunshiny and humid, and then be followed by a cold front. Expect snow tomorrow. Who says the Midwest doesn't have its charms?

I unlocked the door to the sound of the phone ringing. I hurried in and grabbed the receiver. "Ed Darvis Investigations."

"Ed? Bertie."

"Goddamn, you're fast. What have you got for me?"

"Listen up. You got a pen?"

"Somewhere. Got a memory like some animal. I forget which. Shoot."

"Okay, here's the deets. Hanady's first name is Thomas. He's thirty-four years old and chief executive of Limited Imports."

"Trinkets?"

"Naw. Bananas. Has a midwest distribution."

"Ah. I noticed you're using the present tense."

"That's because there's no record of Hanady's death. In fact, he hasn't even been to a hospital in the last year."

"Okay. Back to the bananas. Is that all? Guy makes a fortune on bananas?"

"Judging from the IRS's interest in him, I'd say it could be something else he's importing."

"Drugs?"

"Why not? Hep cats gotta get their tea from somebody."

"What else you got?"

"He's been married to Jerri Hanady for five years. One daughter, Rachel, age five. She was adopted at age two—"

"From Colombia. I know that. No mention of divorce?"

"No."

"Any idea of how often he's in Colombia?"

"Not from what I have so far."

"You got a number for the import shop?"

There was a pause on the line.

"Look, Ed, where's this going?"

"What do you mean? I'll give Mrs. Hanady the privilege of hiring me to recover her daughter. She'll give me a nice retainer, I'll return her bundle of joy, she'll leave her sap of a husband for me—"

"Listen. Those two officers dispatched this morning may be green, but they've already proven themselves capable."

"Sure, Bertie. And I appreciate the show you're putting on for me. Who's listening over your shoulder?"

"Just don't get in their way."

"You know I won't. I'll play very nice and we might even cooperate on the investigation. Now, may I pretty please have that number?"

Bertie gave me the number, as well as the Hanadys' address. These I did write down. "Thanks, buddy, you're a peach." I hung up.

Soon it would be time for the early afternoon pickup across the street; some of the kids stayed until five, and even six o'clock. A rush of wind shook the Bradford pear in front of my window, and the sky turned greyer. Any minute now. The deluge.

I picked up the phone and dialed Limited Imports. A secretary with a perfunctory pleasantness in her voice answered.

"Limited Imports. How may I direct your call?"

"Tom Hanady," I said evenly.

"I'm sorry, he's away. May I take a message?"

"No, thank you. Do you know when he'll be back in the office?'

"I can't say. He's been on a business trip."

"Really? For how long?"

"Who may I ask is calling?"

"This is Barry Whitworth, from Sunny's Grocery, you know? We had some bad bananas last shipment."

"I'm sorry. If you'll wait a minute I'll pull your file." Fat drops began to strike my front window.

"That won't be necessary. If you could just tell me when you expect Mr. Hanady to return, I'd like to speak with him myself."

"Mr. Whitworth, Mr. Hanady is often called out of the country at a day's notice. He should be in touch with us shortly about a return date. I can connect you with our southern district distributor."

I could see this was going nowhere.

"That's okay. Say, how's Mr. Hanady to work for?"

There was a pause on the line during which I could hear a typewriter clacking in the background. The rain complemented the sporadic tattoo of the keys.

"He's a fine man, Mr. Whitworth."

"Well, that's good to know. Hey, I need to get back on the floor."

"Are you sure I can't take a message for you?"

At that moment something outside the rain-streaked window caught my eye. My pulse quickened.

"That won't be necessary, Miss. But thanks anyway."

"Goodbye. Mr. Whitworth."

I hung up and squinted to be sure I was seeing right. A Cadillac had just pulled up into the space next to my car. The driver's door opened and a woman, covering her head with a large purse, emerged.

I hustled to the glass door and pushed it open. She rushed in without looking up. She shivered, her back to me. Rivulets of water dropped onto the linoleum.

"Mrs. Hanady?"

I expected, with a little thrill, to see blue eyes. Instead, as she turned around, I saw beautiful green eyes, sternly examining the office. Her face was nearly expressionless when she returned her gaze to me, but her verdant eyes were penetrating. Then she nodded.

"Please, take a seat. Can I offer you some coffee? I'm afraid I don't have a towel here or anything. Would you like my coat?" I gestured to the rack that held a navy sports coat. This time, she shook her head. She sat slowly, and then she spoke. I was surprised at how clear and resonant her voice was.

"Yes, please. To the coffee, I mean. I don't need a coat."

I unscrewed the cap to the thermos. Luckily, I had a clean, albeit chipped, mug on the shelf behind me. I poured the lukewarm liquid, handed her the mug, and sat down.

"Mrs. Hanady, thank you for coming to my office. I've spoken with Marni Reyes. Did she give you my card?"

She looked at me, her eyes scrutinizing me from an otherwise impassive face. "No. I haven't talked to Miss Reyes. Not since … this morning." She sipped at the mug.

So, she came here of her own accord. That was a surprise. "I spoke with Officer Frederick," she continued. "He said he took a statement from Miss Reyes." Frederick. Officer High-and-Tight.

"So, I take it the police don't have any leads?"

"I don't think so. He wasn't very reassuring, either."

"Mrs. Hanady, I have a friend on the force, a chief inspector, who gave me some information on your husband. I'd like to ask you some questions for corroboration."

She took the news of my poking around with a nod and clung to the mug. "Of course."

"I witnessed what happened this morning. That's how I got involved." I watched her expressionless face. "I'm not technically involved with this case unless I'm hired."

I paused a moment, thinking she would give me the go-ahead. She just seemed to examine the tired grain of my second-hand desk, so I continued. "However, having spoken to Miss Reyes, I suspect something more delicate might be going on. Something that maybe you don't want to tell the police? Or, that they might not be able to help with?"

"I'm sitting here, aren't I?"

"Yes, ma'am, you are. Are you seeking outside assistance in finding your daughter?"

She smiled ruefully. "Yes. And that would be you."

"Okay. Before we go on, I'm afraid I need to discuss fees." I wasn't afraid at all. But the rich like to hear that money pains some people.

"I'll pay any price to get my daughter back."

"My normal fee is fifty dollars a day, plus expenses. That's it. In some cases, the client has to pony up reward money, from which I might get a percentage, but I don't think that's what we're talking about here." I meant to imply ransom, too, and my percentage from that, but I didn't figure she'd handle it well. "Since we're near the end of the day, and if you choose to hire me, I'll waive today's fee and start the clock tomorrow." I smiled to cover the crassness of my last statement. She didn't seem to care. I passed her a sheet of paper scrawled over in turgid legalese. She signed it dispassionately.

"Thank you, Mrs. Hanady. Now, if you don't mind?"

"I'm ready … anytime. But first," she held up her coffee mug and said, "do you have anything to put in this coffee?" I knew she didn't mean milk. Damn. I had killed the scotch.

"I'm afraid not. But look, I can run to the package liquor down the street."

"No, please don't. I shouldn't anyway. I quit last year. Tom hasn't, though."

"Hasn't? Or didn't?"

She blanched.

"Mrs. Hanady, my buddy on the force said that there was no death certificate for your husband."

"No, there wouldn't be. He's alive."

"Did you not tell Miss Reyes that your husband had died?"

"I did. At the time, I couldn't think on my feet." Although I found this hard to believe, I let her continue. "Besides, he might as well be dead."

"Why do you say that?"

"Because the bum is always off somewhere. He's barely in Rachel's life. Not to mention mine."

"I saw a photograph of the three of you at the school. I have to admit you all looked happy."

She grimaced. "That was a happy time. Tom was home more often. Rachel had gotten used to our home, our life. I had quit drinking."

"Was alcohol a problem?"

"It was. I was just…. You see, we had tried for years to have a child. Finally, a doctor told me that I couldn't have children. I was devastated. Tom took it well at first, but then something changed in him. He was travelling at the time, making more trips to Colombia. So, I wallowed in alcohol when he was gone. When he returned, he could see something was wrong. I think he chalked it up to infertility, and that just seemed to sour him more."

"How long did this go on?"

"For several months. But then he came back from a trip with flowers. For me. He took me in his arms like he did when we first married, and I fell in love all over again. Excited by his spontaneity, I asked, 'What? What is it?' He swung me around and said, 'We're going to have a child! We're going to adopt!' I was so taken aback that I cried. He told me all about the opportunity in Colombia, how there were so many sweet children in desperate need of a mother and a father. We shared a bottle of Dom Perignon to celebrate. It was the first time in a long time I'd felt so good."

"When did you make the trip to Colombia yourself?"

"I don't know. Maybe three months later. We'd found out who Rachel's birth mother was, and I wanted to meet her."

"And did you?"

"Yes. She was almost a child herself, barely nineteen. She was so beautiful and shy. It was important to me to see her."

"Why did she give Rachel up for adoption?"

"She's poor. So many of them are. They work on the banana plantations. Many of them live right on the edge of the fields, in shacks. Tom looks for the best supervisors; he really does." An unexpected defensive note entered her voice. "But he can only pay so much himself, in order to turn a profit here in the States."

"I see. Where is Tom now?"

"I thought he was in Colombia. He's been gone the past week. I've been taking Rachel to preschool all this year. It's been very difficult—being away from her while she's at school, that is. But all the other mothers insisted it was a good thing. All of them in the charity send their children there."

"What charity is that?"

"Orphan Care. We raise money to help families adopt children from Central and South America."

"Sounds noble."

She blanched and plunked her cup on the desk, sloshing coffee over the side. "It is. And you don't need to say it like that."

"I didn't mean any harm, Mrs. Hanady. I meant what I said. What I don't get is why you don't have a nanny."

She glanced out at her car, like she was now doubting her decision to hire me. I looked outside, too. The rain was abating. "We have Ella. She cooks for us. Plus, Mrs. Carmody started the preschool herself. She thought it would be grand if our children played and learned together. She's in our group," she added.

"Why here, though?" I gestured to the surroundings, and included my office in the sweep of my hand.

"Because the building and land were affordable. And I know what you're thinking. We're not all rich bitches without heart out in West County."

I leaned back in my chair and held onto my protest.

"Besides, the first kindergarten in the country was in St. Louis. But then, you probably knew that already, detective."

I let the comment slide with a smile. "Mrs. Hanady, does your husband drive a Jaguar?" She nodded. "Is his car missing today?"

"It is. It wasn't in the garage when I returned from the school at noon."

"Are you sure it was him who picked up Rachel today?"

"It had to be. God, who else could it be? Maybe he just returned early. Maybe he wanted to surprise me." She grasped the arms of her chair and looked as though she might leap up any second.

"Mrs. Hanady, just one more question. Have you called his office today?"

She settled back in her chair and frowned. "Yes. They don't know when to expect him." She was looking out the window now, clutching her moist purse.

"Thank you for your time. You can trust that I will do all I can to see that your daughter is returned safely. I have a feeling she's with your husband. In good hands."

"I wish I had your confidence right now."

"Let me make some more calls. The policemen you spoke to today will likely be in contact with your husband's office, if they haven't been already. They will also want to come out to your house."

"To stake it out?"

"To talk to you. And, yeah, to see if your husband, or someone else, returns. If he is back—and I think he is—he'll come home at some point."

"You're right. I know he will." She stood and extended her hand. It was soft, her skin supple with lotion. A sensation I had not felt in a woman's hand for too long. I had to fight the crazy notion that I should bend over her hand and bring it to my lips for a kiss.

"I'll call you later this evening. Say around eight?" She nodded. "Good. Please take care getting home, Mrs. Hanady."

"I will." I held the door as she stepped out into the

diminishing rain and got into the coupe. I wasn't quite sure how those long legs fit in that toyish car and smiled at the thought of examining the mechanics of the arrangement. The rain continued to slacken as she pulled away. I inhaled the scent of her skin on my hand.

4. A BOUT AT BROAD JIMMY'S

I was fairly certain that Tom Hanady had his daughter. Maybe when he picked her up, he parked on the other side of the building where I couldn't see his car. If so, I had no case. One thing, though, trouble was brewing in the Hanady marriage. Nothing as bad as some I've seen. But still, trouble. Which, for me, was fortunate, seeing as I could use a bit of business.

I strolled back to the back room of my office, holding up my hand to my nose. Reluctantly, I washed the scent of Jerri Hanady off my hands in the dirty little sink just outside the tiny john. After I dried them, I smelled the back of a palm: nothing but Lifebuoy. But the disappearance of her scent didn't keep her off my mind. Even before today, she had looked over at my office numerous times. I had even entertained the fantasy that she needed a reason to meet me. Now, she had it, but not because I'm another lonely detective. I told myself, maybe she needed me for something more than finding her daughter. Yeah, and maybe I'll get a swanky office in the Continental Building some day. With a sweet secretary, just like I imagined Tom Hanady had.

I walked back to my desk and propped up my feet. So, Tom Hanady, what is your business? What is it really? Tom was the man of the day. And one thing I wanted—and needed if I was to earn my keep—was to get to him before the police did. I decided to try his office in person. If he wasn't there, then I'd try the Hanady estate. If Officer Frederick was staked out there, I could toy with him a little. Give him some practice giving guff to hard guys.

Limited Imports was in another industrial court on the north side. From the nondescript façade of the building, it looked like it might sit well on my side of town. But the court was not as down-at-the-heels as mine was. At least it looked like someone picked up the litter more than once every other week. I pulled into the parking lot around 5:00 P.M. As I got out of my car, a swarm of employees was leaving for the day. Some of the men loosened their ties and doffed their suit coats into the back seats of the mostly late-model sedans of the aspirational class. Others, women mostly, yelled at one another over the rooftops of their cars, laughing and sharing their plans for the evening. None paid any attention to me. If I hustled, I might catch a secretary.

Inside Hanady's building, a well-lit foyer led to double glass doors. Gilded, no less. Quite a contrast to my smudged assembly-line glass door. Beyond, I could see a reception desk lit from beneath. As if anyone entering the Italian-tiled foyer wouldn't notice it. Behind the desk, I noticed a huge oil painting wrapped in a gilded frame. It struck me as odd that the picture was of dark-skinned workers bent with the labor of packing bananas in boxes for transport, rather than an oil of Mr. Hanady himself. I'd sure as hell get my mug done if I occupied this joint.

Just as I approached the front desk, a woman stood up and switched off her desk lamp. She was slim, just shy of buxom. She wore a smart blue jacket, buttoned at the waist with a matching skirt. Her blond hair was teased up over delicate ears. I started to grow eager for our first encounter, but for some reason she ignored my approach, even though my heels clicked loudly on the terrazzo floor. I like hard-to-get, too.

"Excuse me, Miss?"

"Yes?" Suspicion registered in her face. She stood rigidly with her hands touching the desktop.

I flashed my investigator's badge. "Ed Darvis. Private Investigator."

"Oh. Is everything all right?" she asked, with no noticeable change in her expression. That was interesting, I thought. Usually a guy like me is upsetting to people, and they start racking their brains for any transgressions from their past. Even in a place as ritzy as this one. Still, I had her attention now.

"Not sure. Perhaps you can help me. It seems Mr. Hanady returned home early today and picked up his daughter Rachel from school."

"And that's a problem?"

"Not necessarily—if it was, in fact, Mr. Hanady who picked her up. If that's the case, then everything's fine. If not...."

"Are you working with the police?"

"Yeah," I bluffed. "You know, we'll be sharing information." Which was true, although they rarely shared anything willingly, especially with me. And sometimes they had to beat a few details out of me, too.

"I see."

"I'd like to ask you a few questions, if I may?" I took out a pen and notebook, not unlike the ones Officer Hamilton had used in my office earlier. Seeing these props sometimes puts cagey people at ease. Not that I usually do more than scribble and say "Mm-hmm" as they talk.

"Well, it's closing time." She glanced at a slim wristwatch. "Perhaps you could try again in the morning?"

"I promise I won't take long." I flashed her my fine, even row of teeth. Unimpressed, she reached for the desktop telephone. At that, I chuckled and backed away. I'd have to go soft before I made my press. I glanced over to an Eames chair next to a potted palm and pointed to it.

"May I have a seat?"

"Mr. Darvis, I really must be going. Security will want to lock up the building shortly.

"I promise, I'll be out of your pretty hair before you can say 'import tariff evasion'. Or even 'child labor exploitation'."

That did it. A wry smile appeared on her face. She looked pretty good with it decorating her face. Not as hot as Jerri Hanady, but it was a definite improvement.

"Won't you have a seat, Mr. Darvis?" Her perfunctory tone returned. The same one I had heard on the phone earlier, when I posed as a grocery owner.

"Sure. Thought you'd never ask." I sat, laying the pen and notebook down on a side table. I pulled out a cigarette and lit it.

"Oh, I'm sorry. This is a non-smoking building."

"Whadda you mean by that?"

"No one is allowed to smoke on the premises."

I stared at her.

"Mr. Hanady has allergies. Cigarette smoke is one of them."

"Okay." I held the lit cigarette vertically, looked around for an ashtray, and not seeing one, gave her an inquisitive look. She said, "Here," and walked over and took the smoke from me as though it were a dog turd on a stick. She disappeared around a corner. In her absence, I took in more of my surroundings, with my eyes landing back on the oil painting. Then, admiring the lines of the crafted, wood paneling, I noticed something else. A door. A door, so nearly discreet it would escape the casual inspection of any regular person. A few moments later, I heard a toilet flush.

Then, the secretary returned—with the look of a woman practiced in evasion. You know, tight smile, posture forced into a relaxed look, the suggestion of possessing information you'll never guess or be privy to. Either she could get her shit back together fast, or somebody else was in the back.

"Now, what is it, Mr. Darvis?"

"You asked if I was working with the police. Have they been by?"

"No."

"I see. Any police call?"

She almost seemed to warm up to the initiation of an old, familiar game. Her eyes took on a sparkle.

"An officer did call, yes."

"Officer Hamilton?"

"Yes, it was." The word "was" lurched out, like a car in the wrong gear. "How did you know?"

She gave a little, so I decided to give a little, too, to keep her giving. "He took a statement from me this morning, since I was a witness, and saw what happened at the preschool."

"And what was that?" Composed again, she folded her arms.

"Didn't Officer Hamilton tell you? About Mr. Hanady's daughter?" I raised my eyebrows for effect. If she didn't know, she would expect the worst and might show some feeling. Instead, she studied my face for a moment, like she knew the game was still on.

"Yes, he did tell me. And I don't see what the fuss is about.

Mr. Hanady obviously returned home early and thought he would surprise Rachel by picking her up. I'm sure he's home now. With Mrs. Hanady." After she spoke, she held her left arm up and stared at her wristwatch.

"Has he returned home early by surprise before?"

"He keeps an erratic schedule. Markets change, seasons change. We're used to it here."

"Uh-huh. Has Mr. Hanady behaved strangely lately? Anything unusual—outside of his normally erratic schedule?"

"Not at all. He's very pleasant most of the time."

"Most of the time?"

She uncrossed her arms, took a step toward me, and leveled her gaze. From where I was sitting, her face dominated my field of vision, she got that close. A pretty face. "What is it you want, Mr. Darvis?"

I grinned. "Nothing, Miss. . . ?"

"Brennan."

"Brennan, huh? You know the Brennans in Dogtown?"

"I'm quite sure I don't. I'm a transplant. From Pittsburgh."

"Sure you don't? The neighborhood's right alongside Forest Park. Got its name from a dog-eating tribe supposed to have camped there during the '04 World's Fair."

"What charming tales you must know."

This was all lovely. She looked at me like the old man I suddenly felt like. I was getting quite tired of the game, and now irritated with Miss Brennan's diffidence. I tried to rise from the Eames chair smoothly to get in her face, but I almost lost my balance doing so. I didn't quite flop back into it, but I did wobble. When I managed to stand up straight, I dropped my voice to a guttural register, like a growling dog, and stepped right into her personal space.

"Lookit, lady. You said Hanady was pleasant 'most of the

time'. That means something. What is it?" It was my turn to loom in her face. Only I'm not so pretty up close.

I had let her know this was no longer her game. She exhaled and rather roughly shoved a strand of hair behind her left ear. As she did so, I noticed her hand trembling. "Here are the goods, detective. When Mrs. Hanady calls, it's all I can do to be polite. She is a shrew. I would call her a 'bitch', but then, since I'm in Mr. Hanady's employ, I won't." Her voice came out strained. The smooth tone of voice from the phone became a kvetching teenager's. "She calls. He gripes. And then he spews obscenities after he hangs up. Often he'll leave after that. The next morning, when he comes in, he seems none the worse for it, but I know better. Or sometimes, he doesn't show up the next morning, and we receive word he's in Colombia. He's a sweet man. She's a drain." She looked at her wristwatch. "How's that?"

I couldn't help but smile. "That will do."

"I thought so. Now, will there be anything else?"

"One more question. Just how well do you know Mr. Hanady, Miss Brennan?"

She let the question settle. "Strictly business, Mr. Darvis."

"I thought so." I withdrew a card. "If you have any other nuggets you want to toss my way."

"What else do you like tossed your way?"

Touché.

"Plenty," I said and smiled at her.

"I bet." She leaned in a little. I couldn't help but glance down into her cleavage. She seemed to know I would and held her pose for a couple of seconds.

"Well, if I ever get desperate enough for a gumshoe, I know where to find you." She took a step to the side and gestured towards the front door. "Now, I'm quite sure security is on their way to lock up. I wouldn't want there to be any misunderstanding about your presence."

"How very giving of you."

She smirked and made as if to toss her hair. "Well, Mr. Darvis, must I show you directly to the door?"

"That and more."

"I'm afraid not. It's been a … a pleasure."

"I wish I could say the same."

She walked past me to the door, held it open for me, and glanced quickly behind her. I followed her gaze to the door set in the wood paneling.

"Say, Miss Brennan, where does that door go?"

"Is that imperative for your investigation, Mr. Darvis?" When she saw I wasn't moving out the door, she added, "But if you must know, it leads to Batman's cave."

"Never needed him. Thanks again, Miss Brennan."

"Good evening, detective."

As I pulled out of the parking lot, a few cars remained, but no silver-green Jaguar. Miss Brennan played the evade-and-distract game pretty well. But she couldn't hide a key tell. She couldn't keep her eyes from that hidden door. I'd play the odds and bet my money that Hanady was holed up in that snug little office.

I made for a pay phone. If Bertie was at his desk I might persuade him to stake out Limited Imports. He wasn't. The person who answered might have been the same sergeant as before, and he didn't exactly light up at my name. "He ain't in" was the most I could squeeze from him. I hung onto the receiver a moment. An idea formed. Why not?

I pushed down the handle on the pay phone till I got a dial tone. I pressed "zero," then asked the operator to connect me with the District 2 police station. Another sunny desk sergeant promised, with sugar on top, to connect me with Officer Hamilton. Actually, he said, "Hang on," then let the receiver fall to his desktop with a bang. For ten minutes I listened to not only the music playing for the enjoyment of inmate visitors, but heard an irate woman demanding to see someone named Natty, typewriter keys inexpertly and haltingly tapped, phones ringing and ignored. Finally, I heard a voice say, "Where?" Then, the clunk of the receiver as it was lifted off the desk jarred me back to the reason for my call.

"Yeah, Darvis, what is it?"

Officer Hamilton was annoyed when I related where I had been, but he sounded interested when I mentioned the hidden door. From his hesitation, he also sounded like he was pitching between warning me away, and wanting to know what I had learned. I gave him the whole scoop. And like a good reporter, he ate it up and licked the bowl. With forced reluctance in his voice, he said he would cruise by Limited Imports. I hung up and figured he'd be there in ten minutes to check things out. Too bad he'd be too late to check out the scintillating Miss Brennan. But at least I was keeping the investigation moving.

The stakeout taken care of, I decided to head to Broad Jimmy's downtown. It was nearly 6:00 o'clock, and my body protested its lack of nourishment—of the liquid variety.

Even though I lived in the West End, I liked Broad Jimmy's better than the hoity-toity, three-dollar martini watering holes four blocks south of my apartment. And I sure as hell wouldn't fit in at the north-side bars. White guys like me would be made for a cop or a P.I. right away. Plus, at Broad Jimmy's every now and again I'd stay past happy hour and get to see my Uncle Charles. Since his heart attack two years ago, he earned a desk job at National Freightways. Logically, he says, he's putting less strain on his heart pushing a pencil, rather than toting boxes. One thing, though, alcoholic that he is, his heart attack hasn't slowed down his drinking and smoking. But then, here I was at Broad Jimmy's earlier than he was. By the time I arrived on Locust Street, my tongue was practically sticking to the roof of my mouth.

I opened the tavern's heavy oak door, its white paint peeling, and stepped in. Even in the dim light, I could see that Broad Jimmy was nowhere around, and he'd be hard to miss. He must be in his mid-fifties by now, but he's barrel-chested and thick-armed. He served in the Pacific jungle mess as a Marine, at Okinawa. He still refers to the Japanese as Japs, usually preceded by other endearing terms such as slant-eyed, fuckin', and goddamn. Jimmy reminds me of this story about a guy who trained lions for circuses. One day this lion, who'd been raised from a cub, looks edgy when the guy gets in the cage. As he approaches the lion as usual, suddenly the son-of-a-bitch rears back on his legs and clamps the trainer's head right in his jaws. Enough pressure to be meaningful. Just when the guy thinks this is the end, the lion lets go and backs off a few steps. The poor bastard eases out of the cage and locks the door. Just a warning that time. I wish I knew if that guy ever set foot in the cage again without a good strong whip. Broad Jimmy's like that damn lion. I'd hate to be Jimmy's customer who got a final warning.

As I sat down at the bar, I looked around for Uncle Charles, but all I saw were three other regulars at the far end. I nodded to them, even though we've never exchanged more than a few words. By the time they'd get good and juiced, they just wanted an audience, not a conversation partner. All the regulars get the same treatment. If Broad Jimmy ignores you, that's a good thing. You know you fit in. If he's harangued you, questioned your patriotism, or served you watered-down beer, you better get your suds somewhere else.

Kira Harto, Broad Jimmy's wife, was working behind the bar. Despite Jimmy's tiresome anti-slant rhetoric, he brought his Japanese bride home after the war. Maybe that helps me put up with his pistol-whip bullshit. Plus, I don't mind that Kira is tall, slim, and always wears clingy black shirts with push-up bras that summon your attention, like sweet semaphores. Every lonely guy in the world needs a barmaid who will look him in the eye, bend forward just enough to allow a little peep at the cleavage, and ask, "You need another, hon?" with all the sincerity a man has to have. Kira Harto ain't exactly picture-perfect, but she will certainly do. Her English is rough but decent. And she's untouchable, so a guy gets his jollies with just flirtation. And with enough booze in him, a lonely guy will think he's in the tropics, the hard-working world just a dream outside the heavy oak door, a coy woman keeping his glass full. That is, till he remembers the monster of a man she married, with Semper Fi tattooed on one forearm and a caricature of a Japanese soldier being squashed by a fist on the other.

"What you have, soldier?" she asked as she finally came around to me. Oh, yeah—that little touch is nice, too.

"Gin and tonic. With lime."

She smiled at me in that helpful way, and turned to make my drink. I lit a cigarette and looked around. Now this was more my speed. No gilded paintings and Italian marble, no nouveau-riche pretense here. A few strings of colored lights festooned the mirror above the bar. Below, lined up along a translucent display shelf, bottles in various states of emptiness were illuminated by the white light beneath the shelf. I caught my reflection in the mirror—what the hell, it wasn't going to run from me—and did my usual nonchalant assessment of my looks. I don't look half-bad in this light, I told myself. I turned my head sideways, keeping my eyes trained on my head, and brushed the grey at my temples. Some might say rugged; others bum. I doubt 'distinguished' would figure in on anyone's take. Whatever keeps me employed.

Out of the corner of my eye, I was aware of somebody coming out of the men's room. I looked over and saw George "The Beef" Reynolds. He kept to his feet, placing himself behind the seated bunch at the bar. I've never seen him sit down. Instead, he hangs over his listeners, while they sit, drink, and nod up to him. The Beef will pace behind them, stab his finger at the opposite wall to make one of his many points, and get uncomfortably close to his chums to look them in the eye. Then he lets dramatic pauses turn into an executioner's gaze. The Beef had been a pro fighter, heavy-weight in the late forties. He's maybe two inches shorter and more compact than Broad Jimmy, but my money says he's just as tough. No one would dare suggest it, but I bet lots of us wouldn't mind seeing how the two of them would fare in a ring.

Kira brought my drink with a lime and a smile. I smiled back, savoring the eye contact mixed with the anxious knowledge that Broad Jimmy might be in the shadows glaring at our interaction. Jimmy's rigged a helluva lion's den.

I tuned in to The Beef's boasts and proclamations without looking his way. Today I just wanted a drink and a little female attention, so I played the guy staring at his drink by himself. Most people see this as harmless; others take it as a threat. The Beef probably took it as the latter when he called down to my end of the bar.

"Hey, Gumshoe!"

I looked his way concealing a sigh. "Yeah, George?"

"We're trying to work somethin' out here and need your skills."

That was likely bullshit, but once engaged by The Beef, it was best to take him at his word.

I got off the bar stool and carried my drink in one hand and cigarette in the other. I stood outside swinging range and waited.

"Take a seat," he said. I took one. He likes to be the only guy at Broad Jimmy's standing up and in action.

"What's up?" I asked, though I was thinking, "What's the beef?"

"Simple Simon here thinks you could take me on."

"Yeah?" I looked at Simon, a skinny, towboat deckhand with a poorly trimmed grey beard. His rheumy, wide eyes and nervous smile told me he didn't know what the hell The Beef was talking about, but he was snared and knew it.

He didn't make eye contact with The Beef when he spoke. "Now, George, naw, I never said—"

"Sure, you did. You were thinkin' it, hunh? You can't hide nothin' with those clear blue eyes, Simon."

"No, George, I sure wasn't thinkin' that. Not at all."

"You were. Don't lie to me, Simon." The Beef's executioner's gaze was beginning to protrude through his eyes like darts. The pupils enlarged, swallowing up the silver-blue of the irises. If Simon could see himself reflected, he saw a man about to step off the gallows for a short ride south.

"Hey, Beef," I cut in. Mostly people called him George, but "Beef" has a way of arresting his attention in an animal way.

"Yeah?" He turned his dilated peepers my way. Which—I won't lie—unnerved me.

"It'd be no contest. Just give me a blackjack, some cords to tie you down, and a car running outside with a Tommy gunner to make my getaway when you tear through those ropes."

"That'd be about right, gumshoe." He was mollified, his eyes turning dull again. The silver-blue leached back around the pupils. "You got that, Simon? No matter what this guy'd try, I'd still tear him apart." He returned to me and feinted right and left, then landed—what was to him—a light punch on my right shoulder. For me, it was more like he'd slammed a hammer against bone.

"Ouch, Beef, you're slaying me. I give," I said. I rubbed my shoulder exaggeratedly, but it sure as hell hurt. The Beef skipped around lightly, made as if to punch Simon, too, but Simon threw his hands up in front of him like he was at gunpoint. Then, The Beef laughed. It was a laugh like a machine gun, Rat-a-tat-tat-tat, somewhere deep in his throat. He stopped his antics and slung an arm around Simon's shoulder.

"Ah, Simon. Buddy, I love to fuck with you. I really love it." Simon picked up his beer and tried to smile, but it was more like a wince, and his lips quivered just a bit. I recognized then that a keen sense of hunger was erupting for that mythical bout I'd always wanted to see happen between Broad Jimmy and The Beef. I'd be there. And I'd have a big goddamn blackjack for The Beef.

I decided not to stick around to see what other fun and games The Beef would be up to. Besides, sooner or later Broad Jimmy would come down from his upstairs apartment and assist Kira with the nighttime bar duty. And when he did, she would reign in the flirtation to the occasional discreet wink. Not only that, but The Beef would be sloppy drunk by then. Lucky for him, though, with Jimmy on the premises, he got less belligerent. Which would give Simon the chance to slip out of The Beef's grasp and go home. Wherever home was. The other couple of guys would probably wait around for their part-time drinking buddies, fresh from dinner with the wife and kids, or maybe wait for the second-shift workers who arrived as the night wore on. I'd see my uncle another time. And having been summoned by The Beef, the chance for any peaceful drinking had soured.

I slapped a couple bills on the bartop. Kira was busy examining glasses to rub spots off them. She didn't notice, or care, that I was leaving.

5. THE BIG NAP

I drove home with the windows down to the blessings of the heat and humidity, and chided myself for letting The Beef get to me. The Beef was a nobody now, a has-been, at least as far as his professional career was concerned. But in the bar he haunts, he's the chief spook. And what was that business today? Just to prove he's still cock of the walk when Jimmy's not around? I wondered briefly how Kira could tolerate him. Or any one of us, for that matter.

Home was an apartment above a music store in the West End. That sounds quaint, but quaint it ain't. The apartment itself is okay, but the police should license the muggers in my neighborhood. Also, just three blocks away, women hook on Washington. Anyone picturing tall gals with legs to die for and a gleam in their eye for some schmuck, well, all I can say is they should save their spunk for the centerfold girls. Some of the prosties support drug habits. Others are welfare moms from the Pruitt-Igoe Housing Development, just trying to make ends meet. Occasionally, boys, probably runaways, show up. Whatever the market will bear. Single men, married men, older men with a thing for little boys. The police love to bust those pervs especially. It all gets pretty sick at night. By day, though, you'd never know. Washington's what passes for our garment district.

Shoe sellers, jewelers. Walk down there and you hear the inflected patter of Jewish immigrants, the jingle of silver coins, and the cha-ching of cash drawers crunching down on their feed.

As I opened the door to my apartment, I could hear the jazz trio practicing downstairs. One is the owner of the music store, the other two, I think, are brothers. Nice looking colored guys who blow mellow jazz, which is all right with me, till it verges on bebop noise.

One night, I went downstairs to listen to them jam. They invited me to a back room afterwards for gin and funny cigarettes. I tried to pass off a shallow inhale of the joint, but the resonance of their music, their easy, joshing speech, and the smoke that filled the back room, all made me pretty high. Of course, the gin helped it along. Later, I went back upstairs, getting a kick out of each step I missed along the way, and fried up a batch of eggs. I added spoonfuls of grape jelly to the mix, which was hilarious. I enjoyed the hell out of them. It was a good night, but one I don't mean to repeat. I'd just as soon stick with my world-pitching-sideways gin and scotch.

But tonight, their tunes wouldn't blend with my budding headache. The greasy hamburger still sat hard in my gut. How long was an intestinal guess. I took a shower and peeled an orange, standing while I ate. After I finished, I glanced over at my wall clock: five after seven. I'd told Mrs. Hanady I'd call around eight. So, that gave me very little time to scope out her place.

As I rolled onto Route 40 west, I couldn't help but notice the brilliant sky washed blue by the passing storm. A high upsweep of clouds fading into orange and pink made me think of going west when I was a kid, the one time my father took me on a sales trip. I shook my head at the memory and concentrated on the traffic. I rolled down the window and had a smoke. Maybe Miss Brennan was right. Maybe I'd find the estate lit up with little Rachel laughing and spinning on the lawn in a bright pink dress, mom and dad sipping tall drinks on lounge chairs, fingers entwined, expressions of marital bliss on their faces. Experience told me otherwise. More than likely, I'd see rookie cops parked in plain view.

My suspicions were confirmed when I pulled off the outer road and onto the blacktop driveway of the Hanady estate. At the top of the hill, an unmarked car sat, running lights on, pointed towards the house, which was just visible behind a grove of oaks. One figure was silhouetted in the car. Officer Frederick most likely. I let the Chevy roll back down the driveway in neutral until I hit the outer road, then pushed in the clutch and slowly eased the car a hundred yards down and parked on the gravel shoulder. The trailhead to a nature preserve was right across the road. Convenient.

Before I got out of the car, I assessed the woody incline. Time to go natural. I grabbed my binoculars from the glove box. I also took out my .38. I didn't expect to need it, but experience had taught me that it was better to have it and not need it, than need it and not have it.

The hike through the woods wasn't too bad. It was too early in the year for crickets, but robins kept the treetops lively, and a late woodpecker bitched at me before flying out of view. After about five minutes, I could see a clearing in the twilight. To my right I could make out the break where the driveway stretched up. There, Officer Frederick's car sat, a football field away. I caught chatter from his car radio. Sure didn't sound like a police dispatcher. More like Harry Caray doing play-by-play. Frederick sure knows how to be inconspicuous. Idiot. Even the maid would get wise to his presence in a heartbeat.

I skirted around to the back of the house along the tree edge. This gave me a nice panoramic view. There was the neat lawn, bordered by flower beds with a few spent irises nodding off. The house was a big stone affair with multiple chimneys. Atop one was a plaster mock-up of a stork in a giant nest feeding its young. Tall French doors opened onto a covered porch and ran the length of one side of the mansion. And although I couldn't see it, I imagined the walkway led onto a well-furnished brick patio. There were only two lights on in the upstairs window, and one downstairs, in what looked like the kitchen. In back was a separate garage, done up in the same stone, all three doors closed. One of the perks of money. Tom Hanady didn't have to share his garage, like I did. No one to open doors too wide and scratch your car's finish, or park right on top of you so you had to slide your ass into the driver's seat, while resisting the urge to key the hell out of your neighbor's car's own shabby exterior.

I stepped out of the treeline in the gathering dark and squatted in the hedges. Through my binoculars, I saw the stove through the kitchen window. Something was cooking. A woman, portly, grandmotherly, came briefly into view. She stirred complacently for a minute. I trained the binoculars from her image up to the lighted windows on the second floor. One was covered by a shade. The other revealed books lined up in shelves, what might be a library, I supposed. Aside from the cook, there was no other movement for about twenty minutes. Then I thought I caught a movement in the shadow of the house. I stayed still, but nothing changed. Maybe the plaster stork flew off the top of the chimney to go on night patrol. A dog barked somewhere.

As I got up and walked along the treeline, staying out of any ambient light, the chatter of the baseball announcer from Frederick's radio came through clearer. Moron, I thought, do you not know the meaning of 'undercover'? By this time, though, it was too dark to see inside his car. I paused just then, as the hair on the back of my neck stood up. It felt like the prickles of a too-close lightning strike. Then, I felt the pressure of cold, hard metal against my skull. "Be cool. And don't move a inch," a deep voice commanded.

I stood stock still, arms at my sides, binoculars around my neck. My .38 may as well have been a mile away in a dark ravine, for all the good it did inside my coat pocket.

"Now. I'm gonna talk to you slow so you understand. Get me?"

I nodded with utmost care. The resonant voice came from what seemed three feet above my head. I'd never been accosted by a giant.

"Good. Raise your arms and lock your fingers behind your head like you 'bout to do jumpin' jacks. Only don't do none."

Funny guy. Wary of a hair-trigger, I slowly raised my hands over my head. He pressed the gun hard against my skull, while he patted me down. Rather, I felt a sizeable hand beat my torso and slap my legs. In a split second, I was relieved of my gun and wallet. Next came the binoculars.

A flashlight clicked on. The gun was still steady against my head. Nimble guy.

He chuckled. "A private dick, huh?" Guess the crooks watch police shows, too. "All right, Mr. Darvis." His tone and articulation both changed. "Take a step forward and then turn around *reeeal* slow."

The barrel left the back of my head, and just for an

instant, I thought about some fancy moves. But I wanted to see who—or what—I was up against first.

The night has eyes, they say. This hulking manifestation of night also had a big grin full of moon-white teeth. The man was indeed a giant. Six ten easy. His shoulders would make a linebacker weep. His chest was broad, covered in a tight black material. His pants were black, too, and his clown-sized shoes disappeared into the inky grass.

"Look me in the eye."

I did. He continued to grin. "What say we take a little walk up to the house?"

With my hands still on top of my head, I jerked my head sideways. "How about Johnny Law over there?"

"We won't be needing to disturb him. C'mon. You walk in front of me, and you can be sure I'll be right behind you."

I didn't doubt that. I started up the hill towards the house. "He'll see us, you know."

"Naw. I took care of that."

That gave me my first chill. "Mrs. Hanady at home?"

"Now, what business is that of yours?"

"She hired me this morning. To see about recovering her daughter, Rachel."

"Aw, isn't that nice?"

Pissing off a giant with a gun in my back wasn't too smart. So, I decided to shut up. For a big guy, I barely heard him behind me as we came up to the patio.

"Stop here," he said. He let me feel the gun again, this time in the small of my back. "Turn towards the garage in back."

Up close, the garage was a house in its own right. It had an upper floor—like a carriage house—that is, if your carriage was a limousine and you had three of them.

"Nice place. You live here?" I asked.

The giant made no reply. Instead, he steered me towards a door to the left of the garage doors.

"Open it," he commanded.

I did. Ahead of me, a bleakly-lit staircase led to a landing. The hoss of a man shoved the gun harder into my back and said to march up the stairs. Once on the landing, I had thoughts of making a mad leap over the rail, or turning to plant a few well-aimed kicks at my escort's groin. That would have been a good way to die. Instead, I continued up three more steps. Ahead of me, at the end of the hallway was a big window. Three doors lined the way between me and that only other escape: a plunge through glass to the bricks below.

The giant stopped me right before we got to the first door and told me to face the wall. He walked around me, his gun moving along the small of my back, but then pressing hard into my kidney. When he was alongside me and the door, he removed the gun and leveled it at my midsection. He kept grinning. Now I could see him a little better, thanks to the faux-torchlight near his head. As he knocked on the first door—three times, pause, three more times—his eyes never left my face. And mine never left his. I was a little shocked to see some kind of patterned scarring on his cheeks. The cuts looked deliberate, like tattoos. His hair was neatly kept in little nubs atop his head. And the gun—a beaut of a .45, shining, black. My own confiscated gun and wallet were nowhere in sight, but he had the binoculars hanging rather sportingly from one shoulder. From inside the door, a muffled voice said, "Come in, Meeki." Meeki? Nothing meek about this guy.

Meeki opened the door and gestured for me to enter first. With his gentlemanly wave, I might have been going to see a man about a loan.

Two dimly lit, pale orange shades, ensconced on the wall, gave the room a hunting club intimacy. Typical dark oak panelling. A modest wood desk, fronted by two dark leather chairs. A man reclined in the chair behind the desk. No mistaking it, even in this light: Thomas Hanady.

He looked up at me a little surprised. He relaxed when he saw Meeki looming over my shoulder, gun in his massive grip. Guys who relax with guns pointed at people have never been my type.

"Who are you?" Hanady spoke with a soft, almost adolescent voice.

"Ed Darvis. I'm a private investigator. Your friend here found me outside."

"Snooping around, Mr. Hanady," Meeki cut in. He held up my gun, wallet, and binoculars in one of his big mitts.

"Set those on the desk, Meeki. And keep our Mr. Darvis here covered."

Meeki complied. Hanady picked up the gun, held it up and sighted it directly at me. And then smiled. I didn't. He lowered the gun, opened the chamber, emptied the rounds, and dropped them into his desk drawer. He set the gun back down. Then he opened my wallet. His smile had disappeared.

"So, you are a private investigator, Mr. Darvis. And what brings you all the way out to my humble home?" He picked up the binoculars and peered at me through the long end. His smile reappeared. Sweet man, my ass.

"Your wife. She hired me this morning. After your daughter disappeared."

If Hanady was ruffled by this, he didn't show it.

"She hasn't disappeared. She's quite safe." He set the binoculars down. "I love my daughter."

"How about your wife?"

His face hardened. "That's none of your business."

I took that as a no. "Mr. Hanady, I was hired to help your wife find her daughter. If she's safe, that's good enough for me. But, if you don't mind, I'd like to see her myself."

"No can do. She's not here."

"And your wife?"

"In the house, I suppose."

"You suppose?"

He stood up. "I'll ask the questions here, fuckhead." That voice. A warbly tenor trying to sound hard. I began to feel like I was getting reprimanded by a spoiled teenager.

"Hoss, here … I mean Meeki is your bodyguard, I … gather." I jerked my thumb toward the bozo standing alongside me, but didn't look at him. Instead, I kept my gaze on Hanady. I squinted my eyes and pinched my lips into a smile. More of a grimace, really. Didn't want the son-of-a-bitch thinking I was a pantywaist.

Hanady jerked his hand to his face and clawed at his lower jaw, like a grapple. I wasn't sure if he was trying to control his temper, or if he was thinking of a lively comeback. Eventually, he lowered his hand and his creepy smile reappeared.

"He looks after my entire family. And he's quite good," he added with emphasis.

"Good help is so important these days."

"Isn't it? Well, I think we're through here. I'll have my wife phone you in the morning. Meeki—"

"Why don't I just talk to her now? Since I'm out here and all."

"I don't think so, Mr. Darvis. You've already overstayed your unwelcome."

"Not hardly. Can I get a drink for the road? Long way back to the city, you know."

Hanady hesitated. His youthfulness arose in a flush. My guess was he thought he could put a little muscle on me and clear me out.

"I'm afraid I don't drink, Mr. Darvis."

"That's funny, because your wife said—"

"You sure seem to know us well." He must have given some signal to Meeki, which I missed. Just as I began to swell with professional pride and was about to brag, the back of my head exploded in pain, the room went sideways, and I felt my chin hit the desk. The last thing I remembered was Hanady's face leering at me as he got up onto the desk, then his fist rearing back. Then it was lights out.

6. THE LADY (AIN'T) FROM SHANGHAI

I woke up on my back. All I could make out were fuzzy, dark trees above my head, which felt like it was glued to the gravel beneath me. I tried to sit up, but quickly gave up that idea. Nice and easy, Ed, I told myself, as I raised one of my hands and felt the back of my head. My own precious, sticky blood. I put my hand back down on my chest. All I wanted to do was close my eyes. They felt as if they were weighted with bowling balls. Don't pass out, I told myself.

After a couple of minutes, I tried to sit up again, managing only to raise my head enough to see my .38 lying in my lap. The stem of a dying iris stuck out of the short barrel. Nice touch. I tossed the flower aside. Wincing as I sat up, I opened the gun chamber. It was empty. Of course. I looked around and found my binoculars, the lenses smashed. Meeki probably did that with a big toe. I patted my pants pocket for my wallet. It was there. Not moving my head, I pulled my wallet, brought it up to my face, and stuck my fingers inside. Meeki was nice enough to leave me my money.

I moved my jaw back and forth. Sore, but not broken. Hanady sure didn't have the Meeki strength. I tried to orient myself. Hey, my car. I reached up and grabbed the passenger door handle and pulled myself up. Much too fast. I retched into the gravel. Orange pulp for the ants. At least the burger wasn't bugging me anymore. I panted and spat, leaning against the door, as I wiped my mouth with my sleeve. After a few minutes, I managed to walk gingerly around to the driver's side, using the car for support. It was still night.

Once inside, I leaned my head against the steering wheel and breathed. I raised up and peered into the dome-lit rearview mirror. My left jaw was swollen, purplish and pounding. I swayed my jaw from side to side. 'You are sooo good lookin',' I told my ghastly reflection.

Just then, I remembered Officer Frederick. Even though I wanted nothing more than to go home and flop onto my own bed, I thought I'd better check on him. I started the Chevy, turned around, and pulled a short distance up the driveway. No sign of Frederick's cruiser. And no lights on in the house. It was time to do some hard thinking, and I'd need a little help to do it. I took Route 40 back into town, my car mixed in with a few tired-looking interstate travelers. I stayed in my lane. Mostly. Sorry, bud. I waved at the car as it passed. The driver mouthed 'fuck you' as he gave me the bird. Such redundancy. At the first exit that looked reasonably seedy, I pulled off and found an all-night liquor store.

Later, walking into my apartment, I half expected to see it destroyed. Beat up the private eye and toss his apartment. Send him hate mail, too. But the inside was the same—although the sight of the orange peels on the table sickened me. I held my breath and swept them into the trash. Next, I pulled out a tall glass from the cabinet and filled it with ice. I poured in the scotch and drained away most of it in one gulp. I poured another. I'd sip this one.

I sat down on the couch, waiting, wanting the scotch to hit home, but I knew Bertie Albanese would be wondering about me. Before anything, though, I needed to call Officer Hamilton to see what he knew—and to find out if Frederick was all right.

I dialed the precinct.

"Officer Hamilton, please."

"He's out. Who's calling?" More love from the desk sergeant.

I asked if Officer Frederick had reported. That was a negative. That worried me. I played most of my hand and gave a hazy version of what had happened out at the Hanady place. The desk sergeant was gruff, but responsive. If one of their guys was in trouble, they weren't going to screw around stonewalling me.

Next, I dialed my answering service. The operator told me I had just one call, from a solicitor. If I had a contract for every five solicitors, I could retire.

I got up and fixed a pressed-meat sandwich, and washed it down with some cold beer. Then I wet a towel and laid it across my neck. As I headed back to the couch, I flipped on the fans. Even though I'd left the windows fully open today, the apartment was still stuffy. I leaned back in my armchair to do some deep thinking about my next move, but next thing I new the phone was ringing.

I'm usually a light sleeper, but for some reason I didn't recognize the jangle of the bells as the phone. For a moment I sat there, blinking, trying to clear my head. Still dazed, I picked up the receiver and stared at it. Then I pressed the receiver to my ear and listened.

I knew it was a woman's voice on the other end of the line, but I didn't catch what was being said. At first I thought it was a joke—a woman speaking in a pale imitation of an Oriental accent. Then I got my head together. It was Kira Harto.

"Kira. Say that again. And slowly." I fumbled for cigarettes that weren't on the side table.

"I tell you already, Misser Darvis. You listen or not? Is-s-s The Beef."

"What about him?"

"He dead. Outside our tavern. Come quick."

I swallowed and rubbed my hand over my face. "All right. Give me ten minutes."

I made it to Broad Jimmy's in twenty, my head still throbbing. I expected to see police, and the press, vying for position outside the tavern, but the street was empty, save for a few parked cars. I didn't like the look of this. I took my .38 out of the glove box, thrust a few slugs into the cylinder, and tucked the works into the back of my pants. I pulled on my light jacket, just to cover the gun. Damn. Three in the morning and still probably eighty degrees. My armpits were already good and wet.

I walked up to the heavy oak door and tapped on the dark diamond glass three times. The door opened. If it weren't for the hour and the circumstances, I'd have laughed. There was Broad Jimmy, wearing a bright yellow terry-cloth robe loosely tied over his round, protruding belly. His grey chest hair stood out in a furry ruffle above the knot, and he looked sleepy. It would be easy to discount the power under that robe, but knowing otherwise, I had no trouble keeping a straight face.

"Jimmy." He stared back at me like a sleepwalker. "Ed Darvis."

"Yeah, I know you, asshole. Who do you think I told Kira to call? Get in here."

Jimmy was a charmer no matter what time of day. I

stepped inside and waited for Jimmy to make some gesture. Instead he strode behind the bar and grabbed a bottle of bourbon. It was only then I realized all the overhead lights were on. Maybe it was Jimmy's giant frame in the ridiculous robe that distracted my attention beforehand. I looked around as I walked in to join Jimmy. The walls were a dingy grey, and the ceiling was burnished brown by all the cigarette smoke and dust. A heavy brown HVAC system was perched on a reinforced shelf over one end of the room. I hadn't ever noticed that before. As I walked past the pool table, I saw that the Falstaff lamp above it was turned off, too, which is probably why the pool table's felt looked like pale, dried vomit. As I got to the bar, the colored lights usually illuminating the shelf beneath the bottles of hard stuff were off, too. Seeing the room in that light just might be the first step to getting a guy off the bottle.

I took a seat at the bar in front of Jimmy. I guess expecting he would give me a drink was too much. He took a slug from the bottle of bourbon and then sealed it back up. I lit a cigarette and waited.

"The Beef is dead," he said with a sigh of finality. I read both melancholy and relief in his tone.

"What happened?"

"Someone sapped him in the back alley and then slit his throat. Or vice versa. Either way the job was done."

"Have you called the police?"

He gave me a look like I was a slow learner.

"What the hell for? They'd ruin my business for months. Maybe even do me for good. Nah-ah. I'm hirin' you."

"I'm flattered, Jimmy, but this is a police matter. If we don't report this, you could be charged as an accomplice after the fact—or, at the very least, for obstruction of justice. Hell, it could go the same way for me." I gulped some nervousness back into my gut. Jimmy's eyes narrowed further as I finished. "I'm not interested."

"For a dick you don't notice a lot."

"What's that supposed to mean?" Big man or no, I still had some pride.

"I know who did The Beef."

"Then what'd you call me for?" I was regaining some composure with a lungful of cigarette smoke.

"Because it ain't that easy. Kira!" he shouted, turning to face the kitchen off to the side of the bar. The red curtain parted and out came Kira in some kind of pajama-kimono. As ridiculous as Jimmy looked in the robe, Kira looked sexy as hell in silk. My eyes must have registered this incontrovertible fact, because Jimmy growled at me low and menacing. "Get your hard-on somewhere else."

I said nothing, but loosed a lungful of smoke in the direction of the puke-colored pool table.

"Kira, tell Mr. Darvis what you saw. And no ching-chong crap!" Kira ignored him and looked at me. Even at this hour her face was damn near immaculate.

"You want drink, Misser Darvis?"

"Funny you should ask—"

"No drinks! The goddamn story!" Jimmy's arms flapped in the air, one tattoo on his forearm looking cheap and ink-smeared in the direct light as his sleeve slid up. Kira poured me a shot of bourbon anyway from the same bottle Jimmy had just corked. I fought my usual smile in her presence and slugged the shot. I set the glass down hard, and for a moment only the concussion of glass against wood lingered in the air.

"Now tell it," Jimmy commanded. He grabbed the bottle of bourbon and took a fast drink. He seemed overly nervous to me.

Kira looked from me to Jimmy. She folded one arm atop the other across her chest. Not folded exactly, because her palms lay flat; more like she was summoning some energy— or maybe nerve—to begin. I stubbed out my cigarette and kept my eyes on her. She looked back to me.

"I cleaning the bar top. Jimmy, he go in kitchen."

"Kira," Jimmy growled. He took hold of her shoulder. "Drop that crap!" She snatched herself away from him.

"All right, Jimmy," she said in a tone of affection—laced with poison. "Here's what I saw, Mr. Darvis. George was the last one to go tonight. I woke him up myself. He was mumbling and looked as though he could barely see. But he smiled at me. I remember that. And he muttered something about a fight he threw." Kira paused and looked at me fully. Maybe it was the light, but she seemed to have grown three inches before my eyes. And her English had sharpened, as though a warped record had been straightened. It had a practiced lilt, the consonants crisp and jagged, and the vowels clothed in ice. Even in the stark overhead light, with Jimmy scowling in his ridiculous yellow robe, I couldn't help but stare at her face and bask in this new voice. I could feel Jimmy looking at me over the bourbon. But for once, he was quiet. This was Kira's show, and she had us both by the balls.

"I helped him to the door. I've done that a few times." Kira stopped and shot a look at Jimmy. "And no, he's never made any advances on me, Jimmy. He said good night, and when he opened the door, he looked as though he were making up his mind which direction to go. I decided I should call him a cab; so, I came back in to use the bar phone. I went back out a minute later, but didn't see him. Then I heard him in the alley. He was muttering, half singing. I walked towards the alley, but I heard urine hitting the wall. I decided he wasn't going anywhere, at least for the moment. So, I yelled over to him, 'I call you cab, Beef!' I thought he said 'All right', but it was slurred. I went back inside and closed the door. I kept cleaning. Jimmy had gone upstairs about ten minutes earlier. Pretty soon a cab pulled up out front. I heard a car door slam, then nothing for a moment, then a pounding on our door." As Kira continued, the story picked up speed and the sequence of events tumbled out. "I opened it and saw a cabbie there, looking terrified. 'Miss', he said, 'are you alone?' I told him no and got suspicious. 'Jesus God', he said. Just like that. I've never heard that expression before."

"Go on with it, Kira." Jimmy sounded tired and resigned.

Kira continued. "He wouldn't say anything. He just kept glancing towards the alley. Oh, and he was shaking the whole time. I wasn't about to let him inside." She glanced at Jimmy. "I told him to wait outside. 'Beef around the corner,' I said, and I locked the door to go get Jimmy."

For the first time since I'd shown up, Jimmy seemed to be aware of how he was dressed. He pulled the yellow robe together across his massive chest, and I fished out another cigarette to spare him the embarrassment.

"When Jimmy and I came outside, the cabbie was at the door of his taxi, looking like he was scared out of his wits. Jimmy confronted him in his inimitable style, shall we say."

'Inimitable'—I liked that. I wondered if Jimmy thought he might be getting insulted.

"The cabbie pointed at the alley, but refused to move from his car. Jimmy went into the alley and I followed. That's where we found George Reynolds. On his stomach, a pool of blood circling his head and shoulders."

"And you knew he was dead?" I asked.

Jimmy spoke up. "I've seen death, Darvis. I didn't need a coroner."

"Did you feel for a pulse?"

"Kira did. Gotta hand it to her. I didn't want to walk through his blood."

"Nor did I," Kira began, "and I didn't. No pulse. He was quite dead and warm together. It was a disturbing moment for me." Funny, her face didn't register 'disturbing'. I wondered what she'd seen in her lifetime to be so matter-of-fact about finding a dead man, and for that matter, one she knew.

"Then what?"

"We came back around the building, and Jimmy walked over and asked the cabbie what he saw. I was going to go inside and call the police, but the cabbie stopped me. He leaned in to Jimmy's ear and hissed a few things I couldn't hear. Then he got in the cab and drove off. Jimmy was—" She looked at Jimmy for confirmation, or maybe permission, then simply said, "I couldn't tell."

"Go on and say it, Kira," Jimmy muttered.

Kira hesitated a moment longer. "Scared. He was scared. I've never seen that look on his face. I came over to him at once. Tell him, Jimmy. Tell him what the cabbie said."

Jimmy cleared his throat. The act did nothing for the gravel rattling around in it.

"It was a cop, Ed. Out of uniform, but a cop. A beat-cop, from Dogtown. He came running out of the alley when the cabbie showed up."

"Is he sure?" I spat out.

"Cabbies know faces. And cabbies are friendly with the beat-cops. He said his headlights caught the guy right as he came out of the alley. The guy froze, and then covered his face and ran."

My head raced with questions. "Kira, did you see or hear anything while you waited inside?"

"No. Between phoning for the cab and its arrival, I was wiping tables, running water."

"Jimmy?"

"Nothin'. Hell, I was upstairs, about to go to bed."

I kept my eyes level with his and tried to ignore the glowing bathrobe. "Was anyone else around?"

Kira responded. "Nobody that I could see. But I only looked outside briefly, when I heard George in the alley."

"Who was the last person to leave tonight, Kira? Besides The Beef, obviously."

She thought a moment, seeming to recall the faces of every middle-aged drunkard from the night. For a split second I saw my reflection in the bar mirror. Seeing my bruised and beat-up face, I winced and looked away. Then, Kira lit up.

"I know. Simon. The one George calls—called—Simple Simon."

I flashed back to seeing Simon's uneasy countenance under The Beef's powerful arm earlier in the night. His lips had been trembling.

"You know where he lives?"

"Yeah." It was Jimmy's turn to try to regain control. "He lives in Dogtown, too!" he exclaimed as though on the path to discovery.

"What street?" I asked.

"Ah, he lives on West Park. No. Wait. The other one. Parallel to it. Nashville. Yeah, that's it. Nashville. First block in from McCausland."

"Kira, did Simon leave right before George?"

"No. He left perhaps half an hour before him."

"All right. I'm gonna need to find him and this cabbie. Jimmy?"

"Yeah?"

"You hiring me here?"

"What do you think?"

Tough guy. In a yellow robe, no less.

"I think you are. I'm fifty dollars a day, plus expenses. I'll start today. Today being now."

"Okay. Where do I sign?" Jimmy asked. These are the moments I felt like a life insurance salesman.

"We'll do the paperwork later in the day ... today." I wanted to make sure I didn't get stiffed.

No one said anything then. Kira had sunk back into her own thoughts, folding her arms again. Jimmy planted both his hands on the bar top, his natural propriety rooting him, despite the ridiculous get-up. I puffed on my cigarette, thinking about all Kira had said. That's when Jimmy raised his hand and slapped his forehead.

"What?" I asked, anxious to know what epiphany had come to him.

"Goddamn. George. The Beef. The body! What the hell am I supposed to do with the body?"

Kira's eyes fluttered, but she held still. I glanced from her to Jimmy. None of us had considered what to do with the body—till now. What have we become, if such a thing as body disposal goes to the back burner? I focused on Jimmy.

"Got a spare freezer?" I asked evenly. Jimmy looked at me to see if I was kidding. He turned to Kira, and a slow, deliberate smile spread across her face. She nodded slightly at me. I sucked on the tail-end of my cigarette and gave her the grin I'd been restraining since she walked out of the back room. "We'll need some gloves," I added.

Jimmy's laugh sounded like an old coffin creaking open, then splitting to pieces.

7. SIMPLE SIMON MEETS A P.I. MAN

We wrapped The Beef's body in an old tarpaulin. Sweating and cursing the whole way, Jimmy and I hauled him to the basement freezer. The inside of the freezer felt damn good, and we both lingered with the body for a moment, catching our breath and not looking at each other. Kira volunteered to do hose duty in the alley. By the time we finished, it was dawn. Jimmy was grouchier than usual—which was understandable. Hell, I wasn't so great myself. Besides my throbbing head, my empty gut was begging for a fill-up. I didn't think staying around to wait for a continental breakfast was going to get me fed, so I bid them good morning and promised to come by later in the afternoon. The Courtesy Drive-In on Kingshighway would be near enough to Dogtown, so I headed there.

The restaurant was mostly full with blue-collar guys and a few business types. I sat at the counter, the sunshine beaming through the glass and bouncing off the chrome trim. My stool was still warm from the last customer, but the A/C was already cranked up.

As usual, Carl, the short-order cook wearing his characteristic smudged white apron, was flipping patties and spreading hashed brown potatoes around on the top of the grill. The smell of strong dark coffee mingled with the mouth-watering grease. I ordered a Slinger, extra cheese, and onions. Lois, who has waited on me for a few years now, poured my coffee and moved on to another customer without a word. The "courtesy" is everyone gets treated the same—pour the coffee, take the order, and slap the plate and ticket down in one swift motion. No chit-chat or how-you-doin's. Eat and get out. It suited me just fine.

As I sipped my hot coffee and tried not to salivate at the sights and smells of heavy food, I thought about Kira Harto. Here, like some two-bit Mafioso, I'd spent the morning hoisting a big, dead man into a freezer, and all I could think about was Kira, and her transformation from a broken-English war-bride to a well-spoken, educated woman. I'm sure she had good reasons for keeping up the act inside the bar. I suppose it kept most men at an enjoyable, tense distance. What I couldn't figure, though, was how she connected with a lug like Broad Jimmy? But hell, there's probably plenty about him I don't know, either.

Shaking off thoughts of Kira, I returned to The Beef's death. So much for my middle-of-the-night squeamishness about taking the police out of the equation. The coppers—at least one of them—were already in the thick of it. I didn't know what to make of that. If it was a cop from Dogtown, he had strayed a good six miles from his beat. So, I figured, he was there on his own time. Did he work with a partner? Did he have something on The Beef that necessitated giving the boxer a permanent KO? My stomach churned. A sour taste erupted in my mouth. Whether from the ramifications of this budding case and my part in hiding a dead body, or the coffee I was now slurping, I'd need some rye toast. First to even out the Joe, and next, to decide what the hell I was going to do, since I was now an accomplice in covering up a murder.

At 6:30 I paid my check and left. I took Kingshighway to Manchester and then onto Hampton. I cruised down West Park, went several blocks, then cut over to Nashville. I parked at the top of the last block, just east of McCausland, and got out. The rising sun was at my back as I started down the sidewalk checking house numbers. Jimmy said he didn't know which house belonged to Simon, only that it was on the north side of Nashville. He thought it had blue shutters, but couldn't remember if the cracker box was brick or asbestos shingle. I decided to case each house on the way towards McCausland. As I walked along the street, my nifty detective senses didn't perk up, and I was starting to feel like a boob. I didn't even know if Simon had a car. I didn't know, either, if he was a bachelor and led a solitary river life or had a loud-mouth wife and a brood of squalling kids. Hell, I didn't even know his last name. I'd be better off contacting Bertie Albanese to help me out with this. But I was leery of talking to Bertie, friend that he was, if I had to cover up my involvement in a case that might include a killer cop.

I made McCausland without any sign that I'd nailed the right house. Time to turn around and contemplate a door-to-door. Luck favored me then. A woman in a house dress, her greying hair twirled around curlers, shuffled out of her front door to retrieve the morning Post-Dispatch. I took out a piece of scrap paper and pen and wrote down the nearest house number on it. Then I put on a happy face and called out to her.

"Ma'am? Excuse me. Eddie Arnold." I extended my hand to her. She took it, leaning slightly back, as though I might execute a wrestling move on her.

"Eddie who?" she asked. A line of red lipstick was smeared over her upper lip and crept up toward the short channel of flesh under her nostrils.

"Arnold. You know. Like the singer."

"Oh, yes. Like the singer. What can I do for you, Mr. Arnold?"

"Well, ma'am, I was looking for Simon, you know? Guy with a grey beard? Yeah, I'm foreman for the second shift. He left his keys yesterday." I held up my own ring of keys. "I wanted to drop 'em off to him. Figured he probably had a spare to get home, but still, you know how it feels not to have your keys."

"Oh, sure. I can't stand that."

"Me neither. Like I said, I was just heading home myself, over in Maplewood, just off Southwest, and I thought Simon might need his keys." I gestured westward, smiling big and booming with early-morning, good-guy cheerfulness. She's buying it, I thought to myself, as she cradled the bound paper to her chest. "So, if you could point me to his house, I'd be obliged. I got his address from one of the guys at work, but I'm not so sure."

She looked at the address I had scribbled down. "No, that's not it. You're off by one number."

I rolled my eyes and mumbled something like, Those guys in the shop. I swear! She gave me the missing number and pointed me two houses east of hers.

"That's his."

"Well, I thank you. I'll be sure to tell Simon you helped me out, Miss…?"

"Mrs. Reynolds."

I shook off a chill when she said her last name, but kept my smile on. Reynolds? Probably a coincidence. Surely no connection to The Beef. I turned away and waved again. "All right, Mrs. Reynolds. I'll be sure to tell him. And thanks again."

She said goodbye and headed towards her door.

Just as I got to Simon's front walk, Mrs. Reynolds called to me from her porch.

"Oh, Mr. Arnold?"

"Yes?"

"How about a little song for this beautiful morning?"

I decided there and then to retire the Eddie Arnold alias. Still, what the hell. I gave her the opening bars of "Cattle Call" and then beat a quick retreat before she asked me to yodel. It was a relief to knock on Simple Simon's door. It opened immediately after I heard an agitated voice inside.

"Dick, you're early…" He froze when he saw me. "What the—?"

"Wrong Dick," I said with a grin. His face went pale and he tried to slam the door. I slammed my right palm on the door, and shoved my foot into the doorframe.

"Not so fast, Simon. I just want to talk to you."

"No! Get away from me! I don't want any trouble!"

"Trouble? From me? Not likely, unless you try to slam this door in my face again." I pushed against the door and it gave way to my weight.

Simon backed up into the room and held up his hands. "N-no. Please! I don't want any trouble! I'm not even involved!"

I followed him in and slammed the door behind me. I stared at him evenly, never letting my gaze drop. I think this was the first time I'd ever looked at him straight on. Simple Simon had a face that must have had a rough trip down the birth canal and never recovered. Below his big, rheumy, blue eyes, the rest of his features seemed to melt into his shirt collar. His beard sunk into his receding chin, which disappeared into the collar of his shirt as if it was being sucked into quicksand. And I'm sure he could whistle a fine tune through the gap in his front teeth, which would surely send the ladies running the other way. Despite his weak face, his bare arms were sinewy from river work. Even so, I took another step forward, this time leaning in, my nose almost touching his. The silence stretched uncomfortably. His breath smelled like the dumpster behind the Courtesy. "Involved with what?"

Simon took another step back. "Nothing. I don't know anything. Now go away!"

I held my pose right in his face, despite the rotten smell.

"I've … I've got a gun!" he stammered.

Without giving an inch or taking my eyes from his, I reached down and pulled my jacket aside to show him the .38. Simon's eyes trailed down to my gun.

"So do I," I said, baring my teeth. "But I don't plan to use mine today. How about you?"

Simon looked on the point of collapse. He hung his head, slumped his narrow shoulders. I pointed to a ratty love seat behind him and said, "Sit down. Let's chat. This can be quick, if you cooperate."

Without taking his eyes off of me, he stepped back, feeling for the couch behind him, and plopped onto the seat. He looked up at me like a chastened schoolboy. "Please don't hurt me," he pleaded.

"For chrissakes, Simon, get a goddamn grip."

He looked wildly around the room, sweat pouring down into his beard. I was sweating, too. The house was a hotbox. No air conditioning, and no shade for miles around outside. People around here don't want trees messing with their zoysia, I guess.

I pulled out my cigarette pack and offered him one. He leaned back into the loveseat, hesitant, as if the cig was a gold coin under a viper's ass. Finally, he reached for it. But his hand was shaking so wildly, he had to grab his wrist with his other hand to hold the cigarette still while I lit it. It was all I could do to keep from guffawing at him. Then I lit one for myself and pulled up a cheap cotton-fabric chair across from him.

"Nice place, Simon. You live alone?"

He blew out some smoke in a couple of gasps and coughed at the end. "Yes."

"I'm gonna get right to the point. Your buddy, The Beef, is dead."

"You're puttin' me on."

"Like hell. I saw his body. A brand new smile carved in his muscled neck."

Simon flopped back against the love seat. If he was going to need smelling salts, he was with the wrong guy. I'm only good for a few slaps.

"Broad Jimmy and Kira Harto told me you were the last to leave before The Beef."

"Yeah? So?" he began. "Wait! You don't think I did it?"

"I don't know. But I'm talkin' to you."

"Jesus, buddy. How could—? Could you imagine me trying to cut The Beef?"

"Stranger things have happened. Where did you go after you left Broad Jimmy's?"

"I came home. I took a bus. I swear it! Two buses. I came home and went right to sleep."

"You see anybody around before you caught the bus?"

"No, not really."

"What the hell does that mean?"

"I mean maybe a pedestrian or two. I don't know. Coupla niggers. They all look the same to me." He looked at me half-proud, half-bashful, like he wanted to take a stand against me somehow.

I ignored Simon's bid for racial solidarity. "Where were the Negroes?"

"They passed on the other side of Locust. I didn't really look at them. Animals. You don't make eye contact with them, you know." He puffed out smoke, righteous, his indignance giving him confidence as he sat up straighter. The itch to slap him grew strong.

"Were they all Negroes?"

"Yeah. I swear."

I looked at him over my own cigarette. He couldn't hold eye contact long, busying himself with shaping his ash on the side of a cracked plastic ashtray. "Why did you think I was coming here to hurt you?"

"Because of what happened in the bar. Because of what The Beef said."

I laughed and leaned toward Simon, and with a sinister undertone, I said, "That? That was just The Beef's bullshit."

"You're not gonna hurt me?"

"I already told you, Simp—Simon—I'm not puttin' any hurt on you. Unless you don't cooperate."

"Well, that's all I know."

"What'd these colored guys do?"

"Nothing. They were just shuffling along the street. By the time my bus came, they were gone."

"How about the bus ride? Any reckless drivers? Strange occurrences?"

"I don't know. I was half-asleep. Didn't see a thing."

"Why'd you think I was this Dick guy when I came to your door?"

"Dick's my ride to the landing. He'll be here any minute, too," he added with emphasis.

"Nothing to me." I stood up and gave him one of my business cards. When I leaned over close to him, I thought he was going to bust through the back of the couch into the wall behind him to get away from me. "I'll be in touch. Call me at my office if your memory improves today. In the meantime, not a word. To anyone—police, your buddy, Dick. Anyone. Got it?"

"Yeah, I got it." Simon put his cigarette up to his mouth and took a drag. The man's hand was still shaking.

"And another thing, Simon?"

"What?" he asked, pronounced defiance in the clipped way he snapped out the question.

"Brush your teeth. Your mouth smells like a dead possum."

He closed his mouth and pursed his lips, and his face got hard, but he didn't say anything.

I gave him my winning smile, walked out, and slammed the door behind me.

Back in my apartment I thought longingly of my modest, comfortable bed. I needed to sleep, but couldn't. Not yet. I had to reach Bertie, find out what Hamilton and Frederick had discovered. In my groggy state, I was starting to mix them up, plus now I had a third cop who wouldn't want to be my playmate once I found him. If I was going to probe around into official corruption, I'd need Bertie's trust to do it—and to cover my saggy ass if necessary. I tried his direct line, but no dice. I dialed his home number. I was in luck.

"Bertie? It's Ed. Yeah. Listen, I need to talk to you." I summed up the night's festivities out at the Hanady estate, including that Hamilton and Frederick might be missing, though I left out the new development with The Beef. He said he was going to go in to his office, and that he'd meet me at mine by 10:00 A.M. I debated catching some shut-eye in between. Naw, I could do that at the office.

Another beautiful late spring morning, and already too hot for this time of year. When I pulled into the industrial court, the morning drop-off at the preschool had already commenced. I thought it'd be nifty if Mrs. Hanady was there, dropping off her daughter, but she wasn't. Sure, I'd be out a new case, but she would have her Rachel back. And I'd again get to enjoy the beautiful view from the comfort of my desk.

Inside my office, nothing had changed. Mrs. Hanady's mug still sat on the desktop, a smudge of evaporated coffee on the bottom. I decided to check in with the answering service.

The operator was pleasant. Three messages: two more solicitors, and a Mrs. Hanady.

"What did Mrs. Hanady say?"

"She said, quote, 'Tell Mr. Darvis that I'm very worried that he did not call last night. Please have him phone me immediately.' She also left a number."

I thanked the operator and hung up. I immediately dialed the Hanady place. The phone rang about ten times before I felt myself starting to doze. Finally, I hung up.

I felt woozy. I was worn out from lack of sleep. My headache had slipped into a low throb, thanks to the Slinger, but I'd have to skip the catnap if I wanted to stay on top of this case. I lurched up from my chair and pushed out the front door, intending to walk across to the preschool. If Rachel Hanady was there, I'd have little to do until Bertie showed up.

Immediately, I turned back into my office, as I felt the heft of the .38 against my waist. Yeah, maybe not the best entrée into a preschool. So, I deposited the pistol in my desk lap drawer, then doubled back toward the school entrance.

I entered and found the same receptionist, free of her

Agatha Christie paperback and chips this time.

"Hi, remember me?" I tried a smile. My jaw, still sore, checked that impulse.

"Yes. Mr. Darvis. If you're looking for Miss Reyes, I'm afraid you're out of luck. She took the morning off."

Along with everyone else, I thought.

"The police came by earlier."

"Yeah? The same officers as yesterday?"

"Just one of them. Officer Hamilton."

If Hamilton was okay, then maybe his partner was, too.

"Thank you." I was about to walk out of the building, but then I remembered. "Is Rachel Hanady here today?"

She looked down at a roster. "No, she isn't."

"Any word about her?"

"No. And I'm sorry." She seemed to mean it.

"Okay. Thanks again." I walked out. The sun was spreading down the street, sparking a little humidity. Which didn't do wonders for my headache.

I went back into the office, ransacked my desk drawer for some aspirin, and debated washing it down with some scotch, but then remembered I'd left it back in my apartment. I guessed water wouldn't kill me. But coffee, I thought, was better, so I put the coffee on to brew, doubling the usual grounds.

Waiting for it to percolate, I dialed Hamilton's precinct again, but stopped when a police cruiser pulled in behind my car, lights flashing. I hung up the phone. Immediately, another car, unmarked, screeched up to a halt behind the cruiser. Hamilton, sunglasses on, leaped out from the driver's side. He looked pissed. Then the passenger door opened, and out stepped an officer I didn't recognize. Both of them drew their guns and crept towards my office door. Why they were creeping in full view is anyone's guess. No one stepped out of the unmarked car.

I decided to stay put. They entered one after the other. Officer Hamilton first. And he had his gun on me.

"Stand up!" he commanded. "Hands in the air!"

"What's this, officer?"

"Do it!" shouted the other. I raised my hands, trying to read Hamilton's face. The second cop moved around the desk and brought my hands behind me as I stood. Hamilton kept his gun on me.

"Officer Hamilton, what's going on?"

"Ed Darvis, you have the right to remain silent. Anything you say—"

"Cut that out, Hamilton. What am I being charged with?"

His gun didn't waver until the other cop had the hand-cuffs locked snug around my wrists. Hamilton nodded at the other, who then shoved me forward.

"C'mon, Hamilton, what are you booking me for?"

Pushing open the door in front of me, he shoved me toward the patrol car. He glared at me as if he wanted to spit in my face, but instead spoke in a barely audible growl.

"For the abduction and murder of Officer Jonas Frederick."

8. SWEAT THIS ONE OUT

They led me straight to the sweat room. I'd tried various angles of protest and feints for information on the ride down, but both officers were mum. That is, Hamilton was mum. The other cop took some pleasure in describing what he looked forward to doing to a cop-killer. Lucky for me he waited outside the room while Hamilton and the plainclothes detective, who followed us, prepared their own strong-arm. I needed Bertie Albanese.

Hamilton wore a look of utter rage and contempt. The plainclothes, maybe ten years older, sized me up coolly. They began with the standard question: "Where were you last night?" I started with the drive out to the Hanady place, including seeing Frederick's car in the driveway. I related what I had seen of the house, my run-in with Meeki. And that Tom Hanady was at home and had, in fact, purpled my jaw—with the help of Meeki, of course. The detective leaned over to examine the lump on my head, shrugged at me, and sipped on some coffee. I walked them through the morning, and told them about my plan to meet Bertie.

"He's chief inspector, District 9. He's probably at my office now, wondering where the hell I am."

"Joe," the plainclothes officer said to Hamilton, "go see if you can reach Bertie Albanese."

"Do you buy all this bullshit?"

"I don't know. But Bertie's a good start."

I sighed. Hamilton left the room and closed the door. It was just the me and plainclothes.

"Listen, Detective…?" I waited.

"Marconi."

"Detective Marconi. Bertie and I go a long way back. I used to be police, foot patrol, District 3."

"Yeah? When?"

"During the war." Marconi smiled and passed off a kind of snort. Yeah, I thought, I was an irregular, unfit to serve my country overseas. Don't mention it, asshole. "So, Detective, you ever walk the Bloody Three? In uniform?"

Marconi just looked at me blankly.

"Lookit, Bertie can vouch for me. He also knows everything I know so far about this case."

Marconi raised his paper cup, peered at the bottom, then flung it into the trash, splashing some dregs on the grey wall above the can. "I'm inclined to believe you. But you're staying put until we get a hold of him."

"I expected that." I waited again. "What happened to Frederick?"

Marconi sighed and pulled out a cigarette and lit it. He held another towards me. I wiggled, still handcuffed behind my back. He sort of smiled and put the cigarette back in the pack.

"We know he was shot. Once in the back of the head. That's all it took."

".45?"

He scowled. "Yeah, how did you know?"

"I told you. That's the make that Meeki guy carried. Plus, I just remembered. He said something about Frederick being 'taken care of'."

Marconi shook his head, loosing out a stream of smoke.

"Goddamnit. His face was fuckin' blown apart."

"Where did you find him?"

He regarded me a moment. "In the woods along the outer road, unincorporated West Lou. Two hunters found him."

More guys with guns. "Any witnesses?"

"No." Anticipating another question, Marconi continued, "He was face down. No other signs of violence to his body."

"How did you guys make me for a suspect?"

"Tom Hanady called it in. He said you had been up to the house threatening him."

Jutting my jaw forward, I asked, "Did he mention how he treats his house guests?"

"No. He said that his bodyguard escorted you back to your car."

I grunted at that. "Some escort. Did he mention Officer Frederick's car?"

Marconi was going to respond when Officer Hamilton strode back in. He paused and looked from me to Marconi. He looked like he had stepped into the wrong room. As green as he was on the force, this was likely his first time dealing with a suspect in this way. I hoped to God it was his first and last time dealing with a slain partner.

"I reached Detective Albanese. He'll be down in a few minutes."

"Good. Let's just keep Mr. Darvis in here until then. I'm going to wait outside. If you—"

"I'm going to stay in here, Detective."

Marconi looked as though he were going to say something else, then stopped. He stubbed out his cigarette and left. Officer Hamilton sat in a chair next to the door. He faced me, his seething not yet under control. From the quivering of his lips, I could tell a deeper emotion was threatening.

"Listen, Officer Hamilton—"

"Zip it, okay?" His voice came out in a tremble.

"I'm sorry … about your partner. Jesus, I—"

"I said shut up!" He jumped up, and in one quick stride, fist drawn, punched my sore jaw. The impact knocked me out of the chair, and with my hands cuffed I could do nothing to break the fall. I should have expected this. I don't know that he did. It hurt like hell and I felt my eyes water. He pulled me up roughly and thrust me back onto the chair. The door burst open and Marconi came in.

"Officer Hamilton! Come with me."

I watched as Hamilton followed Marconi like a chastised teenager. Right before the door closed, I heard Marconi growl, "Go to your desk and get some goddamn cof—."

If someone had told me an invisible felon had drilled wet plaster into my brain, I'd have believed them. I couldn't make sense of anything. Except that Tom Hanady had called in and pointed the finger at me. Where was he now?

The door eased open a minute later, and in stepped Bertie Albanese.

"Ed. You look like hell."

"I'm in it. Any chance you could persuade them to take the bracelets off?"

Marconi strode in behind him. He nodded to Bertie and came around behind me. Finally, my blood reacquainted itself with my fingers.

"Thanks, Detective." I turned to Bertie. "Bertie, what's going on?"

Bertie shrugged. "No one's at the Hanady place except the cook. She confirmed that Mrs. Hanady was at the house last night and left early this morning. She didn't know Mr. Hanady was on the premises, nor did she see this Meeki. We dispatched two officers to the house. No cars. We found Officer Frederick's cruiser parked along the outer road."

"Any evidence in Frederick's car?"

"Not exactly. There was a faint chemical smell, though."

"Chloroform?"

"Could be. We think he was knocked out and then shot elsewhere. The highway patrol has taken part in the investigation now."

"What about Tom Hanady? Detective Marconi said he had called in."

Marconi nodded. He took a seat and looked from me to Bertie.

"We think it was him. But he's nowhere to be found."

"Anyone check Limited Imports?"

"Hamilton surveiled it last night. He said the secretary you described left around 5:45."

"With anyone else?"

"Hard to say. She pulled her car to the back of the building before leaving. She appeared to be alone when she left."

"Bertie, I had the feeling Tom Hanady was squirreled away in his office when I spoke to her."

"Could be she snuck him out."

"Does Hamilton know?"

Bertie glanced at Marconi. "No, he doesn't. He followed her for a while and then," he raised his hands, "lost her in traffic."

"Shit," I said.

"We'll have someone out there today," Marconi interjected.

I glanced back and forth at both men. "You think Hanady blew town?"

Bertie sighed. "The way this thing is going, I think he blew the country."

I was released ten minutes later and told to keep my nose out of the investigation. It seems I was still a suspect. Bertie offered me a ride back to my office.

In the car he was quiet and tense. I peered out the window as we passed through a suburban area. Some guy was keeping the zoysia neutered to a harmless carpet in front of his house. That looked like a decent life. What in hell was I doing with mine? An old woman in a house dress scowled as we passed her home and rolled through a stop sign. Yeah. That shook me out of my self-pity.

"Talk to me, Bertie. My brain is mush."

"What do you want me to say, Ed?"

"Anything. As long as it doesn't include my complicity in this."

He looked over at me. "All right. I think Meeki killed Frederick. Under orders ... from Tom Hanady."

"Why him? Why not kill me?"

"Is that your ego talking?"

"It's the pragmatist. I'm deeper into this than Frederick ever was. Unless he got close to something."

"Could be. We'll never know."

"Has anyone reached Hanady's secretary?"

"Not that I know. They've got someone on it, though."

"I think your hunch is right about Hanady."

"Which one? That he blew town?"

"Yep. And I think he went to Colombia."

He looked over at me again. I met his eyes briefly before he made the turn into the industrial court. "I'm gonna find that secretary myself. I want you to stay put until I reach you. Got it? Go home. And clean up for god's sake. You look like shit."

I laughed and said, "Thank you for noticing."

"Seriously, Ed, go home and get some sleep. Take some

meds for your head."

I grinned at that. "What kind?"

He chuckled grimly. "Aspirin. You're too late for a fuckin' shrink."

9. THE DOGTOWN BEAT

Bertie dropped me at my office. I swore I'd go straight home and even made a show of unlocking my Chevy. But as his sedan disappeared around the turn by the welder's shop, I abandoned that effort and went straight into my office. Before I could follow Bertie's sage advice to clean up, I had another mess to take care of. I needed to call the taxi service and find out which taxi driver saw The Beef and then took off. Anyway, who needs sleep? A police roust is always good for the circulation.

I plopped my tired ass into the squeaky office chair and stared at the immense distance between my hands and the phone. Two cases at once. Well, if I did right by my new clients, I'd be able to keep the lights on and buy name-brand smokes. But I was nowhere closer to finding the Hanadys' daughter, or solving The Beef's murder. I was getting beaten around more than I was comfortable with. The list of suspects was growing, and the body count was rising. In actuality, this feast of bloodshed was making my famine diet of cheap liquor and off-brand cigarettes look pretty good.

The squeeze on Simon this morning convinced me he wasn't The Beef's murderer. That didn't mean he wasn't involved somehow. But I also didn't feel bad about muscling him. I needed to show Simple Simon I was tougher than him, and a sick part of me wanted to keep him in his place in the food chain. Meeki had certainly shown me mine. I touched the welt on the back of my head, then ran my hand along my cheek. Hamilton made his bid known, too, on my jaw. It would never be the same. I belched the remainders of my greasy breakfast and picked up the phone.

The operator connected me with Yellow Cab. A dispatcher with a strong St. Louis accent answered.

"Yellow Cab. How can I help youse?"

"My name is Ed Darvis. I'm a P.I., hired to investigate a case involving one of your cabbies."

"Don't know a thing about it."

What'd I expect, a snappy 'yes, sir'?

"The name Broad Jimmy mean anything to you?"

"Yeah, sure it does. This's got nothin' to do with him, does it?"

"Let's just say he'd be very interested in your cooperation in this matter." I lent some goomba inflection to my voice. Sure couldn't hurt.

"All right, I got no truck with Jimmy. This is a union shop, fella. Whadda ya need?"

Bingo. "I need to know about a fare outside Broad Jimmy's last night. After closing time. Who was dispatched there?"

"Gimme a minute."

I heard him set the phone down. Up close to the receiver, some papers shuffled around, then I heard what might have been an industrial fan roaring in the far background. A car engine turned over, then revved. An echo sounded through a cavernous space as the engine settled to idle. The dispatcher came back on.

"Tim Hamill. Name's Tim Hamill."

"Gotcha. And where's he live?"

"He's not in any trouble, is he?"

"Just wanna talk to him."

The dispatcher gave me his address, including the cross street. Tamm Avenue. Dogtown. Same neighborhood as Simple Simon.

"Well, isn't that cute," I said.

"What's that supposed to mean?"

"Nothing. Thanks for the information."

The dispatcher had hung up before I finished. In moments like that, I always want to call back and then hang up after "Hello." The kid in me.

I closed up the office and got back into my Chevy, which had preheated to the seventh-circle-of-hell quite nicely during my field trip with my police buddies. One thing was for sure, before the day was out I'd be needing some cold refreshment, if not a deep nap for my poor sleep-deprived body.

I found Tim Hamill's place on Tamm, right across the street from St. James the Greater Catholic Church. Hamill lived in a flat over a bakery. He had his own entrance, right next to the front door of the bakery. I tried his door, found it locked, then rang the bell. Nothing happened over the next few minutes, even though I rang the bell three more times. Finally, I cupped my hands around my eyes and peered through the glass in the door; then I rapped on the glass, hard. About the time I was going to bang on it again, another door at the landing on the top of the stairs opened up. Geez, another guy in a robe. This one blue.

He took a few steps down, craning his neck to see me. I gave a little wave. He straightened the cord around his waist and continued down the steps in a leisurely fashion. I was sure that seeing my broad tie and jacket, rumpled though it was, he'd probably already made me for a detective. He reached the door and opened it a crack, his face unshaven and expressionless.

"What is it?" he asked.

"Ed Darvis. I'm a private investigator."

"Yeah, so?"

"Your dispatcher told me where to find you."

He stared at me expectantly.

"Broad Jimmy hired me earlier this morning. Seems you were dispatched to his tavern to pick up a body." At the word 'body' he blanched.

"I don't know anything about a body."

"Relax, bud, I didn't mean anything by it. A body. A fare, you know?"

"Let me see some ID."

I shoved my ID and badge onto the glass. He shrugged.

"I'd like to ask you some questions about last night. Can I come in?"

"I don't think so."

"Then why don't you come out on the sidewalk and we'll fry some eggs together." He frowned. I crossed my arms and returned his look. When it was clear I wasn't moving, he sighed.

"Gimme a minute. Meet me in the bakery. They've got tables."

I wasn't keen on discussing this case in public, but I needed this cabbie to be comfortable while I grilled him. At least for now.

I opened the door to the bakery and strode in under a chiming bell. Two overweight women stood in front of the counter, eyeing glazed donuts. A slim, attractive older woman in a gingham apron stood patiently on the other side. Above her, an angled mirror showed off some overly decorated cakes in the lighted display cases.

I nodded my head to her when she looked at me, and she smiled in return. It looked genuine, so I relaxed a little. For some privacy, I took a seat at a round glass table in the corner furthest from the front door. As the two customers continued some dispute about which donuts to get, I pulled out a cigarette and held it to my lips in a gesture of permission. The proprietress shook her head, then returned her attention to the two women. I inserted the cigarette back into the pack and continued to wait on Hamill.

At last he showed up. I had kept my eye on his cab parked across the street, just in case he decided to duck out on our date. He walked in, freshly shaven, hair slicked back, wearing blue jeans and a white button-down shirt, tucked in no less. Some kind of dime-store cologne washed over me as he sat down. He arranged his gangly frame in the chair opposite me.

"They got table service here, Tim?"

He looked surprised to hear me speak his name.

"No. We've gotta order at the counter."

The two women had settled their donut wrangling and were paying up. I offered to get coffee and went up to the counter. The proprietress gave me another warm smile.

"Sorry ye can't smoke in here. It affects the quality of the baked goods." She spoke with a first-generation brogue, not quite Maureen O'Hara, but close.

"No skin off my lungs," I said and winked. She laughed and covered her mouth. I ordered two coffees. In half a minute, she brought forth two steaming cups. I paid her and told her to keep the change. She smiled again. Maybe I should hang up my .38 and sell restaurant equipment instead. Get all the love.

I returned to the table with our coffees. Tim nodded and sipped at his cup, not looking at me.

"All right, Tim. Broad Jimmy and Kira Harto told me you were the one who found the body." I kept my voice low. Some Irish reel was playing quietly behind the counter.

"Yeah, I did," he admitted. "Whose body, by the way?" His abrupt acknowledgement of The Beef's corpse didn't put a wrinkle on his placid face.

"You didn't recognize him?"

"He was face down in his own blood. I didn't do a character sketch."

I chuckled. "No, I guess not. Tell me about the other man. The one who ran out of the alley."

"Aw, man." He brought his cup back up to his lips and blew at the steam rising from it. He looked out at his cab like it was rigged to blow. "Well . . . ," he looked at me and then whispered, "It was a cop. A cop for chrissakes."

"How'd you know?"

"Man," Hamill uttered again. He looked like he was going to clam up.

"Hey, Tim, you're a good Catholic, aren't you?"

"Yeah, so?"

"So, Father Doherty baptized me." I nodded my head towards St. James. "I've been able to help him out in the past. He's been known to look out for me, too." I let Hamill think that over.

"C'mon, buddy. I don't need this."

I leaned over the table and stared at him without blinking.

"All right, all right. He's a local guy. At least, Dogtown is part of his beat."

"What's his name?"

"I'd rather not say."

"Shall we go over to the good father and make a confession."

He didn't say anything; just gripped the coffee cup.

"Or is it you'd rather obstruct an investigation?"

"Downing."

"Hunh? Didn't catch that."

"Downing, Downing. Officer Downing." Hamill slunk down in his seat.

"You know him well?"

"No. Just enough to recognize him. He walks along Tamm Street most nights. He's got a pretty easy beat, if you ask me."

"Why's that?"

"Nothing happens around here. Sometimes kids steal car radios, but everyone knows who does it. He keeps his eyes on a couple of houses in the area. No dads around, you know. One set of lesbian grandmas."

"Lesbian grandmas?"

"Yeah. This boy Bobby, he lives with his older brother, kid sister, and his grandma. She has a live-in woman they also call Grandma, but she's a fuckin' dyke."

The woman behind the counter gasped. I looked over and saw her mouth hanging open. For a split second, I felt embarrassed for her.

"I get the picture," I said to Hamill, "but keep it down. Now, about this Officer Downing. You're sure it was him you saw outside Broad Jimmy's?"

"Positive. That's what makes this so...." He trailed off, at a loss for words.

"Uncomfortable?" I offered.

"Yeah. Say, who was the poor schmuck? The one that died?"

"George Reynolds. You ever hear of him?"

"Don't shit me. The Beef?"

"One and the same."

"God."

"I wouldn't say he's seated at his right hand right now."

"No, I guess not." Hamill sighed. His cologne was nauseating.

"Let me get some things straight. Kira told me you came to the door all nervous. Tell me what you saw."

"I pulled up front and looked around. I wasn't sure about getting out. Sometimes these late-night pickups are a ruse for a robbery."

I decided to test a theory simmering in the back of my mind. The rest of this conversation depended on how he answered this question. "You didn't recognize Kira's voice on the phone?"

"Why should I? I don't hang out down there."

Gotcha, asshole. "Go on."

"I was sitting there making up my mind if I should get out of the cab, when this guy comes wheeling out of the alley."

"Officer Downing."

"Yeah. Him. He was in his civvies, though. He looks right at me, then covers his face and takes off running the opposite way. I thought that was strange to say the least. I got out of my cab, real slow, walked around to the other side, and called out, 'Hello?'" Hamill laughed ruefully. "I must have sounded like a victim in a horror flick. But no answer, and the cop was long gone."

"Then what?"

"I walked over to the alley and peeked around the corner."

"Pretty brave for a nervous guy."

"I'm no punk, mister. That's when I saw the body."

"And then you ran back and pounded on the door of the tavern."

"Yeah."

"Tell me what you whispered to Broad Jimmy."

"What?"

"Kira said you whispered something to Broad Jimmy and then took off."

"Oh, yeah, that. I told him who I saw running out of the alley."

"What for?"

"What do you mean 'what for?' I just saw a dead man. I saw a guy I recognized running from the scene. Wouldn't you do the same?"

"Sure. Sure I would." I glanced back at the counter. The proprietress continually cleaned the same spot on the counter top. It was clear from the look on her face that she was hearing every word.

"Hey, hon, I can't quite hear those pipes well enough. You want to turn that music up?" Without looking at me, she turned the radio knob up and continued cleaning. "Look, Tim," I said in a low voice, "you sure we can't talk in your apartment? I don't keep a clean house myself."

"Hunh? What are you saying? I keep my place clean." His voice was rising.

"Easy, Tim. Nothing personal. I just figured being a single guy, you know, cleaning wasn't at the top of your list." I glanced around and leaned in toward him. "Here's what I want to know. Why were you so specific about the cop you saw? Why not just say you saw a guy running?"

"Look, bud. I saw someone I knew. It scared the hell out of me. I told Broad Jimmy who he was. Figured if the victim lived, he'd tell. And that way, I wouldn't have to be involved. What the hell is so unusual about that?"

"Nothing, Tim. It's all right. One more thing, and you can go back to your beauty rest. Did you tell anybody else about what you saw?"

"Nah. Just you and Jimmy, and the slant-eyed babe."

"All right. Let's keep it that way for the time being. Look. Here's my card. Call any time. I have an answering service. If you think of anything, give me a buzz. I'll probably need to talk to you later." He took my card and shoved it into his shirt pocket. I could see it had about as much value to him as lint. I extended a hand to him and he took it without much force. I tipped my hat to the proprietress. This time no smile.

I got back in the Chevy and pointed it toward my office. As I drove by the bakery, I noticed Tim huddled over the counter talking to the woman behind it. She looked mean, like a mother chiding a disobedient child.

Hamill's story matched Kira's. Except for one important detail, and that was going to cost him. No way he could have heard Kira calling for the cab. That would have been the dispatcher who took her call.

10. EVELYN WEST & HER PLEASURE CHEST

Back in my office, I checked in with the answering service. Three calls, the woman said. Bertie Albanese, no message. Another solicitor. And one from a police officer.

"What was his name?" I asked. I could feel my heart wake up.

"Matt Downing."

"Any message?"

"No. He did say he'd be looking out for you."

"Thanks again." I held onto the phone and thought a minute. I was sure Officer Downing wasn't going to invite me to a pajama party. I didn't like it. I dialed the operator and asked for the Yellow Cab Company again. The same dispatcher as before answered.

"This is Ed Darvis again. I got a question for you. Were you working the night before?"

"No."

"Who was, if you don't mind?"

"Ben Hartog."

"He work most nights?"

"Yeah. He'll be on again tonight."

"Any chance you got his number?"

"Sure. But I'm not givin' it out to you."

That was odd. He had no trouble giving me Tim Hamill's.

"Not even for an investigation?"

"Not unless there's a subpoena."

"Well, in that—"

He hung up on me again. Son of a bitch. I'd have to look up Hartog's number myself. Or maybe I'd wait to call back tonight. In fact, it looked like most of the action would be tonight. It was 2:30 in the afternoon now. I yawned and looked out at the sunny street. I decided to go home and at least get a couple of hours.

I pulled into the cool garage adjoining my building and trudged up the back stairs, desperate for some sleep. The music store below wouldn't be open yet, so I didn't have to worry about any horns squeaking through the floorboards. And the only other tenant on my floor, an artist, kept vampire hours, too. So, no problem there. Ah, sleep, that knits up the ravelled sleep of care. But no sooner had I opened the door and stepped into my apartment than I caught a quick glimpse of a black object coming at me. Right before, that is, searing pain radiated across my shoulder and I collapsed onto the floor. Instinctively, ignoring the pain, I rolled over to my left away from the intruder. I managed to stumble to my feet and swing around just as he slugged me again. Only this time, I deflected the blunt force with my forearm. Now in full attack mode, I caught a glimpse of a man in blue, right before I kicked him dead in the chest. He stumbled back, dropped the billy club, and howled. Then before the young cop could grab his service revolver, I'd fished out my .38 and leveled it at him.

Even though I was still full of adrenalin, I managed, "Nice try," through gritted teeth. Then, keeping my gun pointed dead center at his gut and drilling him with my eyes, I said, "Don't move a muscle." I took a deep breath to calm down, trying not to pant, or shake. The snarl plastered across my intruder's sweaty face suggested he was going to get the better of me. My snub-nose .38 said otherwise.

"There's an arm chair next to you. Take a seat." He looked at the chair, then at the nightstick on the floor, then at me. I smiled, daring him to go for it. Finally, thinking better of it, he complied with my request and sat.

"Keep your hands where I can see 'em." I motioned with my gun for him to raise his arms. He locked his fingers together and rested them atop his head. Smart man, I thought. So, for fun, I decided to see how far I could take this.

"Actually, lay your fingers on your shoulders."

"What?"

"On your shoulders. Like a ballerina." With my free hand, I aped a ballerina stretching her arm and cupping her hand above her head, then bending it down to touch her shoulder. "Like that."

"Fuck you."

"Now, officer. I usually don't make it my business to point my gun at cops. That's likely to get me killed—and I sort of enjoy my life. But in this case, I'll be happy to make an exception." I trained the gun on his forehead and pulled back the hammer.

He shifted his hands down to touch his shoulders. In that pose, he looked more like some stupid collectible figurine than a dancer.

"Start talking."

Although he sat still, he continued to scowl at me from behind rimless glasses, which were crooked on his nose from our tussle. Like most new recruits, he was clean-shaven, lean, muscular. He couldn't have been more than twenty-five. He looked the type to smile at the little old ladies and wave to the kids on his beat.

"You're the one who needs to start singin', shitbird," he spat.

"Tough talk for a man with a .38 pointed at him. What would you do if I put my gun down?"

"Pull mine."

"I was afraid of that. I'll let you keep it for now. But you make any moves and I will shoot you for an intruder." I squeezed the bridge of my nose. "Now, I don't have all day. I'm tired. And I'm missing my beauty nap. And I'm really not so nice when I don't get my beauty nap."

"Looks like you haven't had one in a long time."

That's it? I thought. Hell, the two fat ladies at the bakery gave the Irish maid better than that. Still, I was game to see where this would go. "So, that's the way you want to play it? Okay. I get it." I put the tip of my gun on his forehead, as risky a move as I could make. "What were you doing in my apartment?"

The man didn't blink. "Waiting for you."

"To sap me? That's not real neighborly, Officer Downing."

He raised his eyebrows, surprised I knew his name.

"Your name's on your shirt." Dumbass.

He looked down and flushed. "Wise guy," he muttered.

"Lookit, if I wanted to rehearse dialogue from 'Dragnet' I would've done it last night. Start talking, else I'm gonna get Chief Inspector Bertie Albanese on the line and let you explain your unwelcome presence in my apartment to him. Or else I could just blow your brains out."

His eyes frosted over.

"Take your pick."

That surprised me, but I didn't let on. I reached for the phone on the end table as I pushed my gun harder into his forehead.

"Operator. Yeah, get me the District 9 Police Station."

"All right, all right. Knock it off," Downing said, his voice quaking.

I didn't acknowledge him. "Hello, this is Ed Darvis. Bertie Albanese, please." The desk sergeant let me know in curt syllables that Bertie wasn't in.

"Oh, well, I was just returning his call. What? Maybe he's on his way over?"

Downing broke in. "All right, dammit. Hang up the phone!"

"Sorry 'bout the commotion on my end, Sergeant," I said into the phone as I stared at Downing. "Must be a neighborly dispute next door. All's quiet now. Goodbye." I hung up and gave Downing a playful grin.

"You fucker," he seethed.

"Same to you. That's for sapping me. Next time you decide to get frisky, I might get an itchy finger and fire this little piece." I let this sink in, but I pulled the snub-nose away from his forehead. He was still sitting with his hands idiotically gripping his shoulders.

"Can I put my hands down now?"

"No. And for the last time, talk. I'm all ears."

He looked at his nightstick again. I kicked it behind me and then sat in the armchair across from him. Downing sighed in resignation.

"Okay, fine. Word is you're trying to finger me for a murder."

"Where did you hear this piece of news?"

"That's for me to know—"

"Oh, I think I know. Let's see," I paused, placing my free hand against the side of my head as though summoning a message from the gods. "I'm seeing a deli. No, wait, it's a bakery. And a woman. Scottish. No, that's not it. Irish! And she's reaching for a telephone. And . . . no, she's putting it down, because someone she recognizes just came in. It's a man. Dressed in a blue suit. Wait, no, it's a blue uniform. He's wearing eyeglasses and a friendly smile. Why, it's Officer Friendly! No, that's not right, either. I'm getting another name."

"Son-of-a-bitch."

"No, that's not it. Ah! I got it! It's Downing." I let that sink in.

"That goddamn cabbie."

"Cabbie? What cabbie was that?"

Downing set his jaw. Red splotches crept up his neck to his forehead. I had him. "So, that was you in the alley," I said. Give 'em just enough rope, they'll tie their own noose for you. Downing pursed his lips together and ground his teeth.

Finally, he said, "Yeah, well, I'm gonna be talking to that rat, too."

I walked over, keeping him covered, and picked up the nightstick. "You always let this do the talking?"

"When I have to."

"I figured as much. You might get a bit further with a softer touch, you know."

"Not when my rep is on the line."

"Why did you kill The Beef?" I wanted him off-balance.

Downing leaned forward, but with my gun still on him, he didn't get up. "I didn't kill him. And that's the truth."

"Were you at Broad Jimmy's last night?"

"Yeah. Earlier in the evening. So what?"

"Were you on duty?"

"What do you think?"

"I'll take that as a 'no'. What time did you leave?"

"About ten. I've got a wife at home."

"Lucky gal."

"Nuts to you."

"What were you doing all the way down at Broad Jimmy's?"

"I walk a Dogtown beat; I'm not confined there. Jimmy's is a good place."

"Funny," I said, "I've never seen you there before."

"Well, I've been there." He glanced at my scotch bottle next to the phone. "I'm just not there getting blind drunk every night." I ignored the insinuation and kept at him.

"Why didn't you talk to the cabbie already? Why'd you come after me?"

"How do you know I haven't?"

"You keeping up, officer? You just said you were 'gonna be talking to him, too'."

"Go to hell."

"You either talked to him already, or you didn't. Which is it?"

Downing stayed mum. I opted for a different tack.

"Were you at Broad Jimmy's after hours?" Downing stared back at me. "Look, I'm all for presumption of innocence. Just like you should be. If you weren't at Broad Jimmy's late last night, I'll believe you weren't. But then why would anyone want to implicate you in some has-been's murder? You don't look the type to be into vengeance killings." Downing winced and stiffened. I'd hit a nerve. Sometimes, with a bit of fishing, I get lucky.

"Yeah, well I'm not," he said. "And I already told you. I didn't murder The Beef."

"I might believe you for now. Did you know him?"

"Just from the fights. My dad and I used to watch him."

"He ever give you any trouble?"

"No, like I said, I didn't really know him. Not personally. Just from watchin' bouts." He said that too quickly. It came out like a lie.

"So, tell me then, why did the cabbie put you in the alley? He ID'd you, you know." Of course, he already knew, but I wanted him inflamed at Hamill again, ready to tip on him.

"How the hell should I know? Convenience? The guy's a dope."

"You know him, then?"

He paused, eyeing me, trying to figure me out.

"He lives in Dogtown. I see him on my beat. Guy always gives me the creeps. Pedophile, if you ask me."

I decided to play on his side to see what it could get me.

"His cologne might confirm that observation."

Downing smiled.

"Anyone wears that dimestore shit's gotta have a thing for kids," I continued. "You ever knock him around, just to see what he'd give up?"

Downing stopped smiling, but didn't retort. I changed the subject again. "So, you knew how to find me. What's the Irish gal's name? The one at the bakery."

He again regarded me for a moment. I could see his wheels turning, devising another lie.

"What's it matter to you?"

"I might want to hire her. She had good instincts, calling you."

He sighed. "Mary Hanlen."

I grinned. Gotta hand it to the Irish. All warmth and welcome until you cross one of their thin lines.

"Look, Officer Downing," I said, waving my gun about for emphasis, "I'm in the truth business. I want to catch The Beef's killer. What about you?"

"What do you think?"

"I've been hired to investigate The Beef's murder. If you're clear of involvement, I'll look elsewhere."

While he pondered what I said, I thought to myself, Sorry, Jimmy, too late to keep the cops out of this.

"Tell you what, I'll let you leave. And this little chat will just stay between the two of us. How's that sound?" I picked up and twirled his nightstick. "But I'll keep this as a souvenir. I waved my gun at him. "Go ahead. You can get up. Leave. And if you don't mind, close the door behind you, real polite-like."

Slowly, he lowered his arms, unsure what my real intentions were. I just smiled and kept my gun level on him. No sense in taking any chances. He didn't take his eyes off me as he stood up and smoothed the creases in his uniform.

"Watch your step," he said and pointed his finger at me. I let him have the last word, but kept my gun on him as he opened the door and backed out of it. Hell, he even closed the door all gentle, like he didn't want to wake a sleeping baby.

With Downing gone, I felt my gun hand begin to tremble. I strode over to the door and locked it. I put the .38 into the side table drawer and blew out a breath. Holding a gun on anyone sometimes gave me the shakes. Putting it to a cop damn near gives me the DT's. I breathed deeply to get my composure. But then my rage mounted, at Downing's impudence, at these two cases, at my lack of sleep. I didn't know whether to have a good laugh, or kick a few holes in the plaster. Instead, I erupted into a ferocious yawn. One thing was for sure: I liked to be the guy pulling the plunger on the little silver ball that bops off the cops and robbers, not violently pin-balling between them myself. So, for once I took some advice from one of the good guys—aspirin, and rest. God knows, I needed both. Just then, pangs that could have been hunger chewed at my gut. Or maybe it was just the acids eating what was left of my stomach lining. I decided to ignore the churnings and breakfast on pain killers instead.

I took a shower and gingerly scrubbed the back of my head. Meeki had left me a killer welt. Maybe he had meant to kill me. My right arm still ached, and I had a bruise the size of a grapefruit on my bicep from when The Beef punched me. The rest of my arm felt none better after being sapped by Downing.

I walked back to my bedroom. The alarm clock said 4:00 P.M. I hadn't seen my bed in over twenty-four hours. I didn't even drop the towel or turn down the covers. Before my head hit the pillow, I fell into a dead sleep.

When I woke up, it was getting dark outside. I had that strange disorientation of the mind that wanted it to be morning. If my phone rang while I was knocked out, I didn't hear it. I headed to the kitchen, the damp towel slipping off as I did. Not bothering to pick it up, I brewed coffee and made some toast. My stomach was growling, but I wanted to take it easy. I chewed on the good side of my jaw, letting the coffee soften each bite. The pain in the back of my head was a dull thud now. After I finished a few bites, I lit a cigarette and pretended to enjoy it. Next, I called the answering service. No new calls. I decided to try Bertie again.

This time he was at his desk. He sounded pissed off.

"Ed, what the hell? I've been trying to call you for the last hour."

"I took your advice, Bertie. I've been dead to the waking world. What'd you find out?" I was hopeful for some dish on Hanady, not back-channel chatter on Downing.

"I reached the secretary at home. She played innocent the whole time. A little coy, too," he added.

"Yeah. That must be her thing."

"I did find out where Hanady goes in Colombia."

"All ears."

"Lookit, I get off in a few minutes. Why don't we meet somewhere halfway and have a drink. I can fill you in. In fact, you can buy me a few drinks for all the trouble you've caused me."

"I don't think I could buy enough drinks to cover that, Bertie, but yeah, you're on."

"Wanna do Jimmy's?"

I swallowed. "Uhh, naw. My uncle will be there, good and drunk. We'll have to fight him off."

"All right, where then?"

"How 'bout the Stardust?"

Bertie laughed. "I don't know, Ed."

"C'mon. Louise doesn't have to know."

"She'll ask."

"So, tell her you went to Broad Jimmy's." Dumbass. "I mean Musial's."

"That wouldn't make my wife feel much better about the ambience in either case."

"No matter. It's the Stardust. We'll work the details out when we get there."

The sound of typewriters and the ringing phones filled in the silence; then I heard a sigh. Then the line went dead.

Bertie leaned over the table and said, "Hanady flies into Barranquilla."

"Bar-a what?"

Bertie spelled it out over the noise of the club. "It's on the northern tip of Colombia. Big enough to handle small aircraft."

The four-piece band was vamping while we all waited for the tardy emcee to appear. Cymbals clashed, and the trumpeter laid on the mute—on, off, on, off—like he was masturbating the bell of the horn. A shaky spotlight stumbled upon the emcee as he jumped onto the stage. Dressed in a shabby, sequined dinner jacket, topped off with a bold-red bow tie, he looked like a cross between Jack Benny and a pimp. He brought a hand down to signal the quartet to stop, but they ignored him.

"Go on," I shouted.

Bertie leaned over the table toward me and yelled. "Hanady never flies commercial. From Barranquilla he has access to the banana region. Bananas and cigars and hogs."

"Sounds picturesque."

"Hunh?" Bertie shouted.

I waved a hand and mouthed, 'Nevermind'.

"Gentlemen, gentlemen," the emcee began. He glared at the bandleader, who shrugged and brought his hands down for the band to finish. Smiling broadly, the emcee glanced down to his left and bowed. "And ladies, welcome to you, too. We can't have too many of the fairer sex here." He straightened up and continued. "Tonight we have a very special treat. Now, you'll want to stick around until midnight, 'cause we're gonna have one helluva midnight jamboree. Our Battle of the Burlesque Queens will feature not only Ann Howe, not only Virginia Bell, but also … Oh, boys! Boys!" At that, the emcee withdrew a large polka-dotted handkerchief and exaggeratedly mopped his brow. The cat calls began. "Yes, oh yes! The lady—"

Shouts of joy.

"—with the fifty—"

Wolf whistles.

"—thousand-dollar—"

A lone, plaintive yelp, and then most of the crowd of tipsy rowdies joined in to shout, "treasure chest!"

"Yes, ladies and gentlemen!" the emcee shouted into the mic, his voice distorting. "The lady with the $50,000 Treasure Chest ... Evelyyyyyyyyn West!"

The cacophony transformed into mayhem. Fists pumped in the air, beer bottles banged on the tables, and pure animal yelps filled the room. I smiled over at Bertie and clinked my beer bottle against his. He just shook his head, but his eyes stayed riveted to the seam in the stage curtain.

"Now," the emcee continued, "Evelyn's generously agreed to give all you hungry treasure seekers a little peep, a little eyeful of her doubloons." The emcee leaned his head back and roared with laughter, and then he bent forward and slapped his knee, causing the microphone to produce staticy-feedback. "Whoa! Even the mic is hot tonight, fellas! And ladies, of course," the emcee said, slyly, again leaning down over the stage eyeing a trio of bleached-blonde beauties seated up front. "So, ladies and gentlemen, just sit back, order another round, enjoy another song, and uh ...," he looked side to side as though he were about to share some secret, "I'll just pop backstage and make sure Evelyn and her two breast friends are all ready!" Buh-dum-bum-bum. CRASH!

The band struck up a tango number, the trombonist laying it on especially thick. Men cheered. The emcee peeped through the curtains, turned back with a wolfish grin to the crowd, then slid through the opening. Moments later, the band came to a crashing halt. The curtains parted and the emcee peeked out at the crowd.

"Fellas. Wowee zowee is this gonna be something!"

The band recommenced.

I looked at Bertie's empty bottle and raised my eyebrows meaningfully. As if I needed to twist his arm. I raised my hand and caught the waitress's eye a few tables away. That is, I, along with about ten other thirsty guys. The band played more softly, maybe to facilitate drink orders.

"So, Bertie, tell me about Barawhatever."

"Barranquilla. Plantation life, like stepping back a hundred years. There's a mountain in the neighboring region. Nineteen-thousand feet plus. Named after Christopher Columbus."

"How would that make finding Hanady?"

"Not sure."

"Uh-huh. Where does Hanady go to do business?"

"All over. They have contracts along the coast of La Guajira. Not gonna spell that one. Beyond that, it's forest and foothills, and then the mountain."

"Plenty of places to hide."

"If he's hiding. He may be in what amounts to plain view and think he's safe."

"What else did you find on Meeki?"

"Meeki Osagae. Born in Nigeria, but living in the States since he was four."

"He get the scars in Nigeria?"

"I wouldn't know. His family had to flee Nigeria. Seems they organized against the British. His father led uprisings."

"Geez."

"Meeki is no one to fuck around with, Ed."

I thought a moment. The waitress was detained at a table full of ass grabbers. "Bertie, what do you think Hanady is into? I don't think it's just bananas. And where does the daughter fit in?"

"I don't know. But she's the key."

"I agree. So, uh … where does that leave me? Technically, I'm still in Mrs. Hanady's employ."

"True. If she contacts you."

"No idea of her whereabouts?"

"Nix. She hasn't been back to the estate. Plus, Marconi ordered you to stay put."

"That's why I took a police escort to the Stardust." I gestured to Bertie.

Bertie frowned. "Don't play tough. Hamilton has it in for you. So does Enshaw." I figured he must have been the other cop who rousted me at my office. At this point, I didn't think it was in my best interests to mention Downing's little visit to my apartment. Didn't want Bertie to form an unfavorable impression of my overall relationship with the boys in blue.

"What about Detective Marconi? Does he have it in for me, too?" I couldn't forget the detective who played nice in the sweat lodge.

"He's a buddy. He believes your story, at least from what I can tell. But his first priority is solving Frederick's murder, not looking out for you."

"I wasn't asking to be babysat. Look, Bertie, I need to talk to Mrs. Hanady."

"I won't stand in your way. If you find her, you know we're gonna want to talk to her, too."

"I'm gonna go to the office."

"Right now?"

I turned my bottle upside-down. "This bottle ain't gonna refill itself. Plus, our waitress has other matters to attend to. If you need me, you know the number."

"Yeah, but, uh…." He gestured towards the stage. "The show?"

I smiled down at Bertie as I stood up. "I've seen Evelyn's big, beautiful, Lloyd's of London-insured boobs so many times I could draw 'em from mammary. Ha, get that, Bertie?" I patted his shoulder. "You enjoy the show, though." I dropped a twenty on the table. "That should cover the drinks. There might even be some left over. If you know what I mean."

Bertie avoided my gaze, but there was a glint in his eyes. Might have been the beers, but I doubt it.

I worked my way through the swaths of smoke and the young, laughing and crowing men in their ties and shirt-sleeves, and pressed past a waitress who gave me a neighborly little bump with her behind. Before I got to the front door, I cast a glance back at Bertie. Our waitress had finally found his table. She was smiling down at him, and he was chattering animatedly at her. I slid out the door past the bored bouncer.

11. HELL HATH NO FURY

I snicked a match to a cigarette and drew a deep breath, sucking in the smoke. The air outside was humid but refreshing after the hot, smoky club. My Chevy hadn't moved from where I parked it—a hopeful sign—and I got in, turned the engine over, rolled down DeBaliviere Street, then headed west on the parkway towards the office. As I drove along and checked my rearview mirror, a sometimes necessary habit, I noticed a car a couple of blocks behind seemed to be following me. Probably nothing, but then, that hunch hasn't paid off for me lately. I slowed down, flipped a sudden U-ey on a cut-through, turned back across DeBaliviere, then headed west again, this time on Lindell. As I approached the Washington University hilltop campus at Skinker, I sped up and then slammed on the brakes and doused the lights. I scanned the roadway. Intermittent traffic on Skinker. No sign of the car following me. A bag man loping in silhouette under a street light was all I saw.

Ten minutes later, after my little paranoid vigil, I drove away towards Maplewood, into the industrial court where my bleak little office lay. Occasional street lamps lit the road up and down the roadway. Most of the buildings were dark, except the paperclip factory, which ran night and day, supplying all the world's goddamn paperwork. Which reminded me, I had been neglecting my own.

As I got out of my car, I glanced around to see if I had been followed. I opened my office and decided against turning on the light. I lit a cigarette, grabbed a cold cup of coffee on my desk, and walked over to the window. Just then, headlights shined in the window. I stepped back from the glass and watched as a police cruiser eased by. Were they looking to sweat me some more? Just as the car passed, I caught just a glimpse of a head turned my way, but couldn't see who it was.

I stood there for maybe ten minutes when, Bingo, the cruiser showed again. So predictable. This time it stopped just shy of my car. The driver's door opened. A uniform stepped out, playing a flashlight along the length of the Chevy, then inside it. I still couldn't see if he was someone I knew. He fixed the beam on the front door glass of my office. I held still. Even though it was dark, I didn't know if the cop could see inside. After a few seconds, the beam moved away. The cop got back in the cruiser, put the car in gear, and then drove off slowly.

True to their word they were keeping me close. I sat down at my desk, splayed my feet forward, then let my body slouch down. I didn't like being watched. Feeling hemmed in made me crabby, as well as punk from a few beers and no food.

Just as I reached for the cold cup of coffee again, another set of headlights appeared, weaker and closer to the ground, like a feeble beast crawling to its death. But I sat up at the sound of a gear stretched to its limit before shifting up. Whatever was coming wasn't weak after all. Some other car was zooming down the twisting road of the industrial court, its low-slung lights belying its high rate of speed. As it drew near my office, the familiar low rumble of a Cadillac coupe reached my ears. Son of a bitch. Jerri Hanady.

She screeched to a halt next to my Chevy. I walked over to the door, and just as I pulled it open, she rolled down the window of her coupe.

"Mrs. Hanady?"

"Get in," she hissed.

I walked toward her car and leaned down. "Why don't you come inside?"

"There's no time, dammit. Get in!"

That's when I heard another car barreling up the road, tires screeching.

I jogged around to the passenger side and got in. Before I'd shut the door, she gunned the motor as if she were an Indy driver. I felt like I was crammed into a clown car.

She sped away from the car bearing down on us. Mournful sirens overtook the sound of her grinding through the gears. I looked back to see the swirl of blue and red lights gaining on us.

I returned my attention to Jerri Hanady. "Mrs. Hanady," I said. She didn't respond. "Uh, Mrs. Hanady, that's the law behind us."

"Hang on!"

Before I could even think about hanging on, she yanked the steering wheel to the left, slamming me against the passenger door. The car careened sideways as we shot out onto Manchester Road.

"Damn, lady, hey!"

She glared over at me, jammed the gearshift down mercilessly to turn north on Hanley, and then really opened her up. The cruiser, only a half a block behind us, kept up.

"That son-of-a-bitch! That bastard!" she hissed.

"Mrs. Hanady, who? What's going on?"

She glared at me again. "Tom! He's got Rachel! And he's

… Aggh!" She slammed the gearshift into third and jetted onto the Route 40 on-ramp without looking for oncoming cars.

"Watch out!" I yelled. The driver of the car in the outer lane lay on the horn and swerved just in time to avoid kissing our car. Mrs. Hanady seemed not to notice. She shifted again and swerved out into the fast lane. I stared at her in awe. Then I glanced down at the speedometer. Eighty-five miles an hour and climbing.

To keep my mind off the coffee threatening to come back up, I yelled, "Is Rachel all right?"

"How the hell should I know?" She was on the point of tears. The car rattled as she zig-zagged from one lane to the next. The cop car struggled to keep up. But one thing I was sure of—he would have gotten backup by now. We were going to be in deep shit if we got caught.

She gasped out something and beat the top of the wheel with one fist. With her left hand, she maneuvered behind a truck in the fast lane and then laid on the horn.

"Move, move!" she shouted.

At this speed and with her emotional state, we were inches away from pulling a James Dean. My life wasn't great, but shit, I still wanted to live it. Just when I thought the car wouldn't handle another abrupt lane change, she jerked the wheel, sending the coupe across both lanes, ran over the grass at an exit ramp, and righted the car in time to pass through a yellow light at the intersection. We were outside the city limits.

As she pulled down an alley behind some stately homes, she had the wherewithal to douse the lights. Even though she'd slowed down and we had no guiding light, she continued to rip down one residential street, then another. And another. I assumed—I hoped—she knew where she was going. So, for that, I kept quiet. Besides, like Mrs. Hanady, I was in emotional overload. No sense adding to her reckless disregard for our lives. As it was, my gut was roiling. And if I'd opened my mouth, I would have thrown up. When she pulled onto a two-lane road in a wooded area, she flipped the lights back on and brought the car up to about fifty.

I looked around past the trees still zooming by and studied the road behind us. Then I turned back around and said, "We've lost him." When she didn't slow down, I put my hand on her forearm. "Mrs. Hanady," I said in a gentle tone, "think of Rachel. Please. Slow down." Of course, I was thinking of me, too.

She started sobbing uncontrollably. Her hands slid down to the bottom of the steering wheel, and she hung her head. Thinking she was going to let go completely, I seized the chance to grab the wheel. When I did, she brought her hands up and covered her face. "Mrs. Hanady, put on the brakes." As we slowed, I gripped the wheel and steered us onto the shoulder of the road. Then, as if her anger surfaced again, she slammed the brakes, hard, and I had to throw my hand to the windshield to keep from lurching into it. Finally, the car stopped. I leaned over and turned off the engine, pulled the key from the ignition, and yanked up the parking brake. Then I leaned back against my seat, closed my eyes, and wiped the sweat from my forehead. I realized then that I'd been holding my breath.

I let her cry for a few minutes. Damn me for not packing a handkerchief. I tried a comforting hand on her right shoulder. She let it stay.

"How about I drive?" I said.

She nodded. I got out and came around to her door. When I opened it, she just sat there. "Mrs. Hanady, please." She took my offered hand and I steered her over to the passenger side. I hurried back around the car and stepped in behind the wheel and started it up. As I pulled onto the road again, keeping it to a reasonable speed, I looked over at her. She was staring out the windshield. Blank as a sheet of paper. The car purred and hummed under my touch, and I found I was perfectly at ease driving it despite the circumstances.

She broke the silence first. "Turn at the gravel road up ahead on your left." Her voice was stripped of tone. I found the road and turned. The headlights played off tall oaks and underbrush. A rabbit darted ahead of us and then disappeared to one side. At the top of a rise, I saw a shack.

"Pull around behind it. Just go over the weeds."

I did as she said, then stopped the car and hit the lights, but kept the engine running. I glanced over at her.

"Turn off the engine."

I hesitated before following her order. Our friendly cop could still have found us. And I didn't like that I had no idea where the hell we were—making a getaway a crap shoot.

We sat for a minute in silence. There were no sounds outside the car. Maybe it was the absence of squealing tires and the roar of internal combustion altering my sense of hearing, but it seemed as though the insects were holding back their racket, waiting, watching us.

"Mr. Darvis, get out. We need to get out and walk."

She opened her own door this time. I came around to her and offered an arm, but she nudged it aside. "Wait here." She stepped onto the porch of the shack. The shack was so old it could have dated to slave times for all I knew. These grounds might have once been worked by forced labor. The thought was not a consoling one. Mrs. Hanady pulled something off a window sill. A flashlight. She shined the beam on a foot path that led further up the incline and began to follow it. I walked behind her.

We went this way in silence for about five minutes. Up ahead I could make out the blue-black space of a clearing. The tall, wide silhouette of a building framed the night. The Hanady garage.

She led me to the back of it. She produced a key and opened a door, then started up a set of stairs. I followed her again. My nervousness returned. My last visit here hadn't been exactly pleasant. At the top of the stairs, she opened a door. And there we were, in the same ugly hallway I had been pushed into before. Only this time, we were on the opposite end. She walked forward and opened the door to Tom Hanady's office. And me without a gun.

Now composed, she entered and flipped on the lights. The same dull orange exuded from the ensconced lamps, but the two chairs in front of Hanady's desk had been shoved out of the way and overturned. His desk sat at an odd angle from the back wall. A file drawer was open, and papers were strewn around on top of the desk.

"Drink?" she asked as she walked over to a cabinet.

I'd never seen a woman go from hysterical to deadpan indifference in such a short period of time. I didn't know if I should be appalled or impressed.

"Yeah," I said. "Yeah, I think I better have one. Pour yourself one, too." She looked at me coldly, then produced a bottle of bourbon and two crystal glasses from the shelf. I walked over to Hanady's desk and noticed a half-empty glass sat on the desktop. I picked up one of the chairs and sat it upright. I watched her walk back over to me. In the orange light, she looked like an overcooked sunbather. I had never seen her so much as unkempt outside the preschool. But now, her brown hair was disheveled, and I saw a line of grey along the part. Dark lines of mascara ran from under her eyes, giving her the appearance of a ghoul. Her blouse was rumpled and stained over one breast. Her skirt, non-descript and a little baggy, was a far cry from others I'd seen her wear. She didn't seem to notice, or care. She handed me a glass and sloshed some liquor into it, then poured one for herself and gulped until the glass was empty.

"Easy," I said. I took a slug from my own glass and watched her. Then I righted the other chair and gestured for her to sit down.

"Now," I said, "tell me what is going on."

By way of reply, she grinned sickly and pulled a folder from off of the desk.

"Read it," she muttered. I set my glass down and opened the folder. As I did, she pulled out a cigarette and bit it between her teeth, then lit it like she wanted to hear it scream. Her sick grin in the match light transformed into a sadist's leer.

Inside the folder were three sheets of paper. I glanced at each one. The first two pages were typewritten. The third was handwritten. On all of the pages, there were four columns. In the first column, there was a list of male and female names, all English. In the second column, all in Spanish, full names were listed. From what I could tell, the first names in this column belonged to women. Next to several of those names were superscript numbers. In the third column, alongside each row of names, dates were entered. In the last column, more dates, between eight and ten months after the dates in column three. Some of the spaces in the last column had N/A scratched in. I looked over each page and then looked at Mrs. Hanady.

Since she'd sucked the life out of the cigarette, she mashed it out. To my surprise, right on the top of the desk. Then she reached for another. She handed one to me and I took it.

She lit mine, and then hers. First time for everything, I guess. For a few minutes, the smoke from our cigarettes congested the air between us. At last I spoke.

"These look something like birth records."

"Oh, really," she deadpanned. Menace oozed from her.

"Well, the dates at the end are about nine months after—" Her seering look cut me off.

"These are Colombian women?" I asked. She nodded. "What's with the numbers?" The sick grin appeared again. She pointed her cigarette to a slim journal on the edge of the desk. I picked it up and opened it. In the same neat handwriting, columns of numbers were followed by notes. I flipped through the pages. The numbers totalled twenty-seven. I picked one at random: number fourteen. I read:

This was a sweet one. Tight, Tight, Tight! Tho she didn't make a sound the whole time. I wanted her to call out in Spanish, like #11. Now she is worth going back for!

I skimmed through a couple of others. More of the same. One in particular, though, chilled me.

Weepy. Weak. Sickly. Might produce a hump-backed calf. No good in the States. Not even worth a roll in the hay. Off the farm! One for Meeki's men.

Throughout, women were rated accordingly. Like a seed catalog of lasciviousness. I closed the cover and held on to the journal. I didn't want to be here in the first place, and now I felt my skin crawl as though in a preemptive getaway.

"Mrs. Hanady. I don't know what to say."

She glared at me. In the orange light, her features were sharp, like the blade of a machete. "Girls! Young girls!

Innocent. God!" She threw her empty glass across the room. The glass shattered against the wall. Then she stood up and grabbed a handful of papers off the file cabinet and made as if to rip them to shreds. Instead, she threw them at me. "Fucking men!" she screamed. At first I was stunned, but when she reached for the tell-tale folder next, I grabbed her hand and stood up. She slammed her other hand down in a fist on mine, then she clawed at my chest like a drowning cat. I held onto her arm and tried to grab her other flailing arm. She landed a couple of good scratches on my face before I could restrain her.

"Mrs. Hanady, I don't like the idea of hitting a woman, but I will." At this, she slackened, so I let go of her. "We need to take these documents to the police."

"And what the hell will they do?"

"I don't know that you are aware of this, but they're working on the murder of a police officer. He was here . . . at your house last night."

She stiffened. "What are you talking about? Murdered?"

"Officer Frederick. He was staking out your house."

"I know that. But how? I thought he simply left."

"I guess you could say that. He was shot in the head and dumped in the woods."

"Oh, God, no." I grabbed her as she collapsed and set her in the chair. I stood over her, in case she fainted.

"The police thought I did it. At first, anyway. Some of them still do."

She looked up at me in horror. I could see she was struggling with the possibility of being here with me—a possible cop killer.

"I can tell you I didn't kill him. I was here." I bounced my finger up and down. "Right here. In this room. With your husband and Meeki." At the name, she snorted. "Meeki hammered the back of my head, and then your husband punched me out. I woke up in the gravel next to the road below." Her expression didn't change. "Mrs. Hanady—"

"Stop calling me that!"

"All right. Jerri. We need to go to the police. You're in enough trouble for outrunning that copper back there."

"I want you to go find him."

"Who?" I said stupidly.

"Tom. I want you to find him."

"I'm afraid that's impossible. I can't leave the state, much less the country."

"I don't care. I'll pay you anything to do it. I'll give you anything to do it." She reached desperately up to her breasts. I felt like I was going to vomit.

"Mrs.—Jerri—I'm still a suspect in Officer Frederick's murder. I have strict orders to stay put, and that's what I'm going to do until I can clear my name. Then…" I trailed off.

She looked up at me expectantly. "Then you'll get him?"

"I'll do whatever I can within reason to bring him in. And, most importantly, bring your daughter back safely."

"Yes. My daughter." She hung her head and whimpered, then just as quickly sat up and steeled herself. She looked straight up at me, her eyes again hard and cold as granite. "I want you to kill him."

12. TRANSCONTINENTAL SHOWDOWN

I've never added killing as one of my qualifications on my resume. I wasn't prepared to do that now. I persuaded Mrs. Hanady to go with me into the main house. The cook embraced her and began fussing over her. I took advantage of this mothering to get to a phone in the den. Turns out the phone wasn't necessary. There was a banging on the front door followed by "Police! Open up!" It sounded like Officer Hamilton. I got up to answer the door, but the cook beat me to it. She looked accusingly at me before opening the door. I stood a few steps behind her. At that moment, I couldn't see Mrs. Hanady.

Hamilton lurched in, bristling for action, gun drawn. Behind him, I saw another cruiser come ripping up the driveway and plunge to a stop next to Hamilton's car. Officer Enshaw jumped from his vehicle and headed toward the door, while Hamilton, ignoring the cook, trained his gun on me and snarled, "What the hell are you doing here?"

"Let's say I was abducted," I said.

"Put your hands up."

I still held the folder and the journal in my right hand.

"Put your hands up."

"Officer Hamilton, you're gonna want to look at this." Still, I held one hand up, but raised my other hand holding the papers as an offering. About this time Enshaw came in. The cook looked disapprovingly at all of us, then returned to the kitchen.

"Ma'am, come back here," Hamilton ordered.

The woman didn't stop. "I got a stew on that I gotta stir," she called back.

Enshaw looked questioningly at Hamilton, who shook his head. "Cover him," Hamilton barked. Enshaw eagerly complied. Hamilton jerked the folder from me and went to sit on a divan. He flipped through the loose pages. His expression betrayed neither understanding nor confusion. Next, he opened the journal. His face reddened as if he'd been caught red-handed reading porn.

"What is this?" Hamilton asked.

"Those dates on the pages." I pointed to them. "They mean anything to you?"

Hamilton looked back down at the paper. The returning redness revealed they did not. He looked back up at me.

I put my hands down. "The first column contains only first names. Notice they're American. Those are the children. The second column contains Spanish names only. Those are the mothers. The third column indicates the dates Tom Hanady slept with the women. And the fourth…."

"Birth dates," he said dully.

"On the money. I think Tom Hanady's cashing in on their adoptions. His daughter Rachel is proof the process works. And … is appealing to men with certain tastes, and who don't want the law worrying after them."

"Jesus."

I noticed an absence. "Where's Mrs. Hanady?"

His slack jaw closed on the words. "She's here?"

"Yes. I'm assuming it was you in hot pursuit of the Caddy? She's the one turned Highway 40 into the Autobahn. Her car is parked on the other side of the property. She was just in the kitchen."

Hamilton turned to Enshaw. "Get her in here." Enshaw strode toward the kitchen, his gun still in his hand. I heard him exchange words with the cook. In a moment he was back.

"She's gone."

"What the hell?" said Hamilton.

I looked at Hamilton. "I know where she went. If you'll follow me, I can show you. We might be able to catch her." He stood up reluctantly. I led the way and Hamilton and Enshaw followed me. I didn't know if their guns were still at the ready, and I didn't care. I figured they were curious enough not to shoot me in the back. Outside, both officers snapped on their flashlights. I led them behind the garage and down to the footpath that ended at the shack. Before we could walk ten paces, the familiar roar of Mrs. Hanady's sports car engine rolled up the hillside.

"We're too late," I exclaimed. "C'mon. She'll have a head start."

"Where are we going?" asked Enshaw.

I thought a second. "The airport. I've got a bad feeling I know what she wants to do."

The officers exchanged quick glances, then Hamilton said, "Let's go." We ran back toward the house, around to the front. Enshaw jumped in his cruiser and tore out before Hamilton and I reached his car. I opened the passenger door and got in. Hamilton said nothing to this but flipped on his siren and took off after Enshaw.

As we reached the outer road, Hamilton picked up his radio and communicated with the police dispatch that we were in hot pursuit. "Adam-Eight, Adam-Eight, code 10-50. Repeat, code 10-50." He gave the make, model, and color of Mrs. Hanady's car, and a physical description of her as well. I stared at the lit blacktop road ahead of us and said nothing. We reached Route 40 and punched it going east. At Lindbergh Boulevard, Hamilton careened around the clover-leaf exit and floored the car northward toward the airport. There was little traffic. Despite the high speed, Hamilton drove smoothly. Good thing, too. My gut still wasn't in the best shape. He blew through every red light, and accelerated through every green one.

We reached the outer road along the airport and continued speeding toward the terminal. A mix of prop drone and jet roar washed over the car. Ahead, we could see Enshaw burst from his car and run up to a man dressed in coat and tie: Detective Marconi. They conferred as they watched Hamilton's cruiser bump the curb and come to a stop. Hamilton was out of the car before I could open my door.

Marconi turned to Hamilton and me. "Go to the Trans World desk. Enshaw and I will cover the other airlines."

"You got any more backup?" I asked. We needed more than four men to search the terminal.

"Coming," said Marconi. "We're dealing with the Sixth. Let's move it."

We badged our way through the lines. No one scrutinized them. We gave each agent a description of Jerri Hanady. None had seen her. Several minutes passed with more of the same. We walked out into a waiting area. Enshaw joined us.

"No luck?" he asked.

"No," Hamilton said flatly.

"Let's find Marconi," I said. They followed me, seeming to accept some authority I normally didn't own with cops.

He was ahead, at the counter of some puddle-jumping outfit. When he saw us, he gestured for us to hurry it up.

Just as we approached him, we heard the agent say, "Yes, sir. I told you already. I'm positive it was her."

"Has that plane taken off yet?" Marconi asked.

"Not yet, sir. But it's due to taxi any minute."

"Which gate?"

"C-18. Just down this concourse."

Marconi started running and we followed. For a guy about my age, he was swift. We reached C-18 just as an agent was closing a door to the outside. Out the large window we could see a two-engine prop plane. One of the tarmac guys was rolling the staircase away from it. Marconi flashed his badge, saying there was a wanted woman on the plane. The agent moved aside and we ran through the door onto the tarmac. Marconi kept his badge out and hustled toward the men rolling away the staircase. "Police!" he shouted. "We need to get on that plane!" The workers seemed to get him over the engine noise. As they rolled the staircase back in place, Hamilton and Enshaw waved their hands in the air up at the pilot to cut the engine.

I bounded up the stairs behind Marconi. Hamilton and Enshaw were hot on my heels. At the top they both clamored for me to get out of their way and let them on first. We stepped onto the plane past a cute, and surprised, stewardess. The plane was small, but full. Hamilton and Enshaw pushed past me. As I passed one businessman, he snarled, "What's going on here?" Another up ahead complained, "I've got an important—" Hamilton told him to can it. A couple of children were giving their mother a squirrelly time of it. We scanned every passenger as we all four walked down the aisle. By the time we got to the back of the plane it was clear: no Jerri Hanady. The plane was smaller inside than it looked from the outside. And all faces were turned on us, some now more amused at our haplessness than annoyed. I'd have suggested we give "Sweet Adelaide" the barbershop treatment if I thought the cops could hold a tune.

I turned and headed toward the cockpit. The annoyed passengers were still muttering. One business type, already a few cups in, called out, "Let's get this goddamn bird off the ground!" The stewardess up front was smiling at them sweetly, but concern showed in her eyes. I asked her if she had seen a woman that fit Jerri Hanady's description.

She furrowed her brow slightly and then the smile returned. "No, I'm afraid not, sir!"

Ah, if only I had the leisure to take a seat right here and let this beauty wait on me all across the continent. Instead, I tried the captain next. He was standing at the front of the plane, his blue cap centered squarely atop a sculpted mask of blue-eyed, glinting American muscle and bone. On one crisp collar, the golden pilot's wings strained to escape their pinning. On the other, some type of combat ribbon rested with valiant restraint. His authoritarian manner reminded me of Broad Jimmy.

"There's no one of that description," he said preemptively. "Now, I need you gentlemen to exit the plane. We are behind schedule as it is, and we're flying against the wind."

Can't argue against grim determination spiffed up with epaulets. I stood at attention, gave him a stiff salute, and exclaimed, "Safe to fly, sir." His eyes narrowed at me but he said nothing.

Marconi, after pushing past Hamilton and Enshaw, joined me up front, grim-faced. He gestured to the door, and we all exited the plane.

Back inside the terminal we found two other officers and Bertie Albanese. As Detective Marconi filled Bertie in on Jerri Hanady's disappearance, I studied Bertie's face. He had dark circles under his eyes, probably just like mine, but he looked alert. I added the sordid details of Tom Hanady's business life.

"Shit. Think Mrs. Hanady's on another plane?" he asked.

"Fifty-fifty," I replied. "If so, that was pretty damn smooth."

"All right. Let's find out if other flights connect to Colombia. Also, I need men to get a hold of the women in Hanady's charity. See if they've spoken to her, seen her, anything. Also, I want a stakeout at the Hanady home. And maybe not in plain view this time? I need someone at Limited Imports, too. What am I missing?"

No one said anything.

Bertie grunted. Marconi sent Enshaw and Hamilton back to the Hanady estate. The other two officers who had come with Bertie would head out to Limited Imports, after checking on other flights that might connect to Colombia. Marconi would start the rounds of the charity women. As we went outside the terminal, I asked Bertie if I could hook another ride with him back to the office.

"Let's not make this a habit. I'll start charging you for gas."

"Deal."

Bertie started the car and we headed back south along Lindbergh. The next three minutes of silence felt like half-an-hour.

"I have an idea," he said.

"Shoot."

"I don't think Jerri Hanady got on a plane."

"Okay," I said, "Why not?"

"Think about it. She's upset. Murderous, even. She finds out what her husband's into, and it destroys her. She cries awhile. Then her emotions rocket to revenge, and she makes up her mind to find you. She's driving blind. Figuratively, of course. She gave the other coppers a helluva chase. She takes you out to her place in a fury. She has to know at some point the police are going to show up. When they do, she ducks out her back door and makes for the airport."

"A ruse?"

"You bet. A damn good one at that. Look at us."

He had a point. "Think she's that smart?"

"Who knows? I wouldn't put it past her. And she's just gotten the burn of her life."

"Convince me."

"I think she knows where her husband is. And he's not in Colombia."

I looked over. "Bertie. Better skip my office and head straight to the secretary's place."

"You read my mind."

13. WHERE GUN PLAY LEADS

Miss Brennan lived on a quiet street in Richmond Heights, an inner-ring suburb. Bertie doused the car lights and parked up the block. He checked his service revolver, then opened the glove box and withdrew his backup .38. He held it out to me.

"Now that's my style," I said.

"C'mon. Let's head up the alley behind the house."

"Want to call for backup?"

"We don't want a landing party just yet."

We cut through a sideyard to the back alley. There was only one street lamp, so we kept to the shadows pretty easily. When we approached Miss Brennan's one-car garage, Bertie risked turning on his flashlight. Shucks, no Jag. Instead, a late-model Ford sedan, most likely Miss Brennan's.

Bertie clicked off the light, and I followed him through the chain link gate to the backyard. Postage-stamp sized, it was neatly ordered with flower beds on both sides. We stayed to the left and softly approached a window facing the back. Both Bertie and I chanced a peek inside. The room, dimly lit, emphasized the outline of one massive man sitting on a wooden chair in the doorway, his back turned—Meeki Osagae. Bertie looked over at me, his eyes betraying his thoughts—'That is one gargantuan man'. I raised my eyebrows in acknowledgement.

Looking again into the room, we saw a bed next to the door and a night light on the opposite wall. In the bed a small form lay, covered with a blanket. Only the back of the head was visible. If that wasn't Rachel Hanady, then it was time for me to retire.

Bertie gestured for me to follow him up the breezeway to the front of the house. I felt my hand clenching the .38 by reflex. As we neared the front, we stopped to peer into the side window. Although a shade had been pulled down nearly all the way, we could still see into the room. A table lamp lit the wall, providing the sole illumination. In the armchair next to it, Miss Brennan sat smoking. Guess she allowed that in her own house, if not at Hanady's office. We could hear a man talking, but we couldn't see him. The even tone, emitted in a steady tenor, broke, and he began shouting. Shit, I thought, somehow he's seen us. Instinctively, I started to push Bertie into deeper darkness. He pulled away from me, never taking his eyes off the window. When I looked back inside, seeing that Miss Brennan's expression hadn't changed, I blew out a sigh of relief. She took another drag off of her cigarette, stubbed it out in the ashtray next to her, then folded her arms across her chest. The man came into view and stood over her, pointing a finger that held a burning cigarette. He wore a white button-down shirt, untucked, sleeves rolled up, tan arms exposed. Well, well, well. The pitched, high voice should have tipped me off in the first place. Tom Hanady.

Ashes from his cigarette fell onto Miss Brennan's skirt. She didn't flinch. Even though his words were clearer now, what amazed me was that she seemed undaunted by his rant. When more ashes fell, she merely unfolded one arm and brushed them from her skirt. Considering who she was dealing with, I thought she was one ballsy lady.

Before I could continue to admire Miss Brennan, I heard the definitive clicking of heels on the sidewalk. Bertie and I ducked down against the house. We raised our guns, ready to defend ourselves, but the heels clicked up the front steps and then we heard the door open. I raised up and looked back inside. Tom Hanady stood with his finger still pointed at Miss Brennan. She was no longer relaxed. Now she sat on the edge of her chair, both hands on the arms, as if ready to bolt. Both looked at the front door. The unmistakable look of astonishment—and fear—registered on their faces. A muted female voice came into the room, and they both raised their hands into the air. Tom began backing up.

"Bertie!" I whispered harshly.

"Yeah," he said.

We bolted for the front door.

Just as we reached the porch, we heard two snaps from a small-caliber revolver. A woman screamed. I stood to one side of the doorframe and yanked open the screen door. Bertie leveled his gun and burst into the room. I rushed in behind him, the .38 pointed dead ahead.

There stood Jerri Hanady, a gun hanging limply from her hands. In front of her, Miss Brennan, her eyes wide with shock, stood frozen, like Lot's wife on a dress rehearsal, her hands still in the air. Tom Hanady lay on his back. He tried to brace himself up, but fell back, pain overtaking him. He moaned as a dark circle of blood grew from his groin, while another flowered across his chest.

Bertie yelled, "Police! Drop the gun!"

Mrs. Hanady's gun fell to the floor with a thud. Miss Brennan, finding her voice, started screaming. I came around Bertie and grabbed the weapon. Tom Hanady was writhing now, croaking, his lips twisting in agony. I stood back up, but stopped. Across the room, Meeki Osagae filled the hallway door.

The giant wore the same grin as the night he sapped me. His hideous scars were muted in the low light. Under one of his bulging arms, he held Rachel Hanady, unconscious and slack in his grip. In his other hand, he trained a black .45, right at Rachel's lolling head. Her eyelids fluttered, then closed again.

"Mrs. Hanady," began Bertie. "Step to one side." She didn't budge. With his gun steadily trained on Meekie, Bertie said, "Ed...."

Never taking my eyes from Meeki, or lowering my own gun, I pulled Jerri Hanady back with one hand and coaxed her down onto a love seat. Her numb expression did not change. Miss Brennan, still wild-eyed and trembling, collapsed into the armchair beside her. She clutched at a glass on the table next to her and sipped, looking up at Bertie and me, as though for permission. She spilled some of the drink on her shirtfront, but didn't bother to wipe it off as she put the glass to her lips. Tom Hanady had fallen unconscious. His shallow, rasping breaths barely blew out of his gaping mouth.

I glanced side-long at Bertie. His face was hard. I knew he was assessing the situation, performing mental triage, even as he stared straight ahead. Everyone, it seemed, was waiting to see what would happen next. Which gunman would make the first move. Everyone, that is, who wasn't unconscious and bleeding or catatonic.

Finally, Bertie spoke, his tone dull, quiet. "Your boss here is going to die if we don't get an ambulance."

Meeki's grin deepened. "What's that to me?"

"No boss. No job. No pay."

"That don't matter now. You see, I got the girl." Meeki bounced Rachel's limp, little body beneath his arm.

"Yes, you do. But why don't you give Rachel to her mother. Then we can talk."

Meeki let out a resonant laugh. "I don't think so. She's coming with me."

"Where to?"

"Bar-r-r-r-anquilla!" Meeki said, with a firm trill.

"What good is she to you there?" Bertie asked. He shuffled forward slightly, passing off the move as a shift in posture.

"She may be a calf now, but she'll be of age one day. Plus, I got me a new boss." Meeki grinned widely. He was just full of grins. Anger swelling inside of me, I pointed my gun at his head. Just one bullet. That's all I needed. "Tom Hanady," he spat, shifting Rachel's weight on his hip, "Tom Hanady? Man, he's small potatoes. He started somethin', but now we got investors."

"What do you mean?" I cut in. Meeki looked at me, looked into my gun.

"Man, we got guys with elephant guns. Hell. . . ," He started cackling, "we got guys with elephant dicks."

"What do you mean?" I asked again. "Mob guys? Local thugs? Or just plain jerk-offs?"

He ventured another laugh. "I tol' you, dick-tective—investors. They got such a plan. You know how much it cost to adopt? We got all the locals tied up. Money come in through them. Money come in through the girls, spreadin' for green tissue. Money come in for drinks, rooms, live entertainment. They got a whole industry goin' down there! Tom Hanady? He was just,"—and in a mock upper-class tone—"the cahtalyst."

"You know you're not going to leave," Bertie said.

"Ha. I know how you want to play this," Meeki said. "But it ain't gonna work your way. I'm taking the girl and we're going out the back door."

Jerri Hanady stood up. She walked by me, zombie-like, nudging my gun hand. "Mrs. Hanady. Jerri. Don't," I commanded. She kept moving forward, her arms out in front of her as though she were caressing the air.

"Stop there if you want her to stay alive," Meeki said, his grin gone. Jerri Hanady fell to her knees, feet away from Meeki. No sooner had she doubled over and started sobbing, than Bertie's revolver flashed. A shrill ring pierced my left ear. Meeki's gun hand jerked away from Rachel Hanady, and blood spurted from his upper arm. Rachel slipped out of his other arm onto the floor. Then Meeki used his good arm to raise his gun hand back up at Bertie. Just as he pulled the trigger, I snapped off a shot and hit the side of Meeki's neck. Blood spurted sideways. Bertie buckled and fell to the floor next to me. Without thinking, and before Meeki could squeeze the trigger again, I advanced on him fast, firing continually at point blank range. Spatters of blood erupted from his chest, dousing my gun hand. One bullet hit his mouth, crushing his awful teeth. As I fired the last bullet, his idiot eyes rolled back in his head and he slumped into the hallway.

I stepped over the prostrate Jerri Hanady, still rocking back and forth, still wailing, and still oblivious to her daughter lying cock-angled against the wall. The room filled with thick, acrid gunsmoke, and the sickening smell of blood. I kicked Meeki, even though I knew he was dead. Then I knelt down and felt Rachel Hanady's neck. She had a weak pulse. Bertie. I hurried over to him—ignoring Miss Brennan who was about to go in full-throttle hysterics. "Shut up!" I yelled as I knelt down next to Bertie. He looked up at me, pleading. He pressed his hands against his mid-section. God. Gut shot.

"Bertie? Bertie!" My voice seemed layered in vacuum cleaner noise, which actually was Miss Brennan, her screams battling past the ringing in my ears. I yelled at her again. "For God's sake, shut up and call for help!"

Bertie's glazed and questioning eyes found mine. I whipped off my coat and pushed it against his hand covering his abdomen.

"Bertie. Hang on. You're gonna be all right." I looked around wildly to see Miss Brennan. When she saw the look on my face, she jumped for a phone. "Hurry, dammit!" I screamed as I looked back down at Bertie. "Hang on, buddy. Hang on."

Out of the corner of my eye, I saw Jerri Hanady finally crawl out of her stupor and pull her daughter gently from the wall and clutch her to her breast. Sobbing, she rocked Rachel back and forth. Miss Brennan hung up the phone and knelt next to Tom Hanady. She cradled his head on her lap and began rubbing her hand over his forehead and cooing to him. He looked as good as dead.

What a scene we must have presented as the police stormed into the room, followed by the ambulance attendants, once they were cleared to enter. Three people bent over ones they loved in the settled gunsmoke and the pooling blood. A lone giant crumpled and shattered at the end of the room.

14. DOUBLE DOWN, ONE DIME

The whole neighborhood was drawn to the spectacle of lurid yellow crime-scene tape and parti-colored lights flashing off the windows of parked cars and housefronts around Miss Brennan's bungalow. So many fire and police vehicles crammed the narrow street that I flashed briefly to our ridiculous grouping in the airplane earlier. This time wasn't so funny. Nearly half the former occupants of Miss Brennan's bungalow needed medical attention.

We were all parceled out in separate rides. Tom Hanady and Meeki Osagae had a date with the Medical Examiner. Miss Brennan was taken to the police station. Rachel Hanady and Bertie were loaded into separate ambulances. Mrs. Hanady and I hooked a ride with officers Hamilton and Enshaw. It took ten precious minutes to shift around the emergency vehicles and locate a few dumbstruck homeowners to move their goddamn cars out of the way so Bertie and Rachel could get priority.

Then you had the onlookers to keep pushing back. At one point a little colored girl in a bathrobe, steered around by her father, stared at me through the window of the police cruiser, wide-eyed, open-mouthed, absorbing my image with a child's guilelessness. For reasons I can't explain, it took everything for me not to cover my face. By the time we all reached St. Mary's hospital, Miss Brennan was most likely under intense interrogation. Rachel and Bertie had been whisked into the ER. Mrs. Hanady and I were relegated to the ER Waiting Room. Officers Hamilton and Enshaw stood grimly on either side of us, looking tired, already jaded, despite their youth. Detective Marconi went to get some coffees.

Fortunately, Rachel Hanady had only been drugged, the doctor—a woman of fine, handsome features—advised Jerri Hanady. "We won't know with what, until the drug tests come back," the doctor said. "Once she's stabilized on an I.V. drip, she'll be taken to the Children's Ward. You can see her now, if you like."

Officers Hamilton and Enshaw, exasperated in the delay getting her to the station, started walking Mrs. Hanady a bit roughly toward her daughter's room. Detective Marconi stopped them. "Give her some time. She's not going anywhere." Marconi handed me a cup of coffee and motioned for me to take a seat. He sat down beside me. He was a pal and took my statement right there in the waiting room.

"Forensics will see if the bullets from Meeki's gun match the round that killed Officer Frederick." Marconi's manner told me it was likely a foregone conclusion. And, at this point, as long as I cooperated, the Frederick murder was an open-and-shut case before the people of the state of Missouri, and I would be cleared. I was probably off the hook.

After Marconi finished with me, he gave Hamilton and Enshaw the go-ahead to retrieve Jerri Hanady and take her to the station.

As they brought her out into the waiting room, both with a hand on her elbows, I got up and stopped in front of them. "Jerri, I'll come in to see you. Tomorrow morning, okay?" She nodded at me, her face blanched, but now fully aware of what was going on. I thought it was nice that someone, maybe a nurse, had the decency to wipe away her black, caked mascara.

As the officers escorted Mrs. Hanady to a waiting car, I paced the floor and sipped the black coffee absently. There'd still been no news about Bertie. Detective Marconi and I watched the business of the ER comings and goings—a howling boy holding his arm, led in by his distraught mother; two nurses hustling through the swinging doors as a 'Code Blue' sounded over the intercom; an irate man with a large belly poking out from under a way-too-small t-shirt leaning over the admitting nurse's desk, giving her a hard time. I felt Marconi's eyes on me.

"All right, Ed. Let's hit it. I'll give you a ride," he said.

I was about to launch another joke about taking rides from police officers, but not knowing Bertie's status, I didn't have it in me. Instead I said, "I'll take the bus. I want to wait for Bertie's prognosis."

"You think I don't wanna know, too?" he asked. His hard manner caught me off-guard. He turned to interrupt my line of sight with the nurse's station. "We've got two pre- cincts worth of worried cops. We'll get news when we get it. C'mon with me."

I didn't know if this was shift's-end crabbiness, or a prelude to further questioning, or what. Something in his manner told me not to disagree. "All right. Let me just drop my card at the nurse's station."

"Fine. Don't try to pick her up."

I nodded and made a brief visit to the seated nurse. After extending her my card, she handed me a paper towel to wipe the crusted blood from my hands. As I walked back to

Marconi, his agitation manifested again. He began chewing a thumb nail and tapping his foot. When he saw me, her wheeled around to leave. I followed him out through the sliding glass doors.

"You okay?" I asked.

"Yeah. It's just fuckin' hospitals." He didn't elaborate, and I didn't press. Sometimes the wise detective keeps his questions to himself.

When we got into his unmarked car, he said, "Where to?" It took me a minute to gather my thoughts and remember just where the hell my car was.

"My office."

It seemed like a month since I'd seen my bed. Truth was, only about eight hours had elapsed between waking up from my dead nap earlier in the evening and stepping back into my apartment now. The time on my wall clock was 3:30. That was A.M. The past two days seemed to be compressed into one long sleepless, bloody episode. But I knew if I didn't eat before I crashed, I'd be through. So, I cracked three eggs into a hot skillet and made white toast. As the eggs cooked, I decided to try my luck on another orange. It was so sweet that I gobbled up the other two on the counter while I flipped eggs and buttered toast. I ate standing up. I knew I wouldn't make it to my bed if I sat down. Afterward, I lit a cigarette, and this time didn't have to pretend to enjoy it. For dessert, I grabbed my tallest glass from the cabinet, plunged in some ice, and topped it off with the rest of the scotch I had bought, when? Last night? The night before? It would sort itself out later.

I carried my scotch into my room. I didn't bother to turn on the light. Out of habit, I found my bedside table in the dark. I set the glass down, kicked off my shoes, and unbuttoned the top of my shirt. I stopped and took one more slug of my drink. And that was it. I was gone.

I woke up with a start to full daylight. As I sat up, shirt and pants still on, I rubbed my face. A final nightmare image of Meeki's scarred cheeks and laughing teeth filled my vision until they exploded in blood spray and bone fragments. I slapped my face and felt something like consciousness. My alarm clock showed 8:30. I stood up and headed into the kitchen. God, I needed coffee.

While it brewed, I called St. Mary's. Bertie Albanese was still critical, but stable. They'd taken him to surgery to repair his intestines. The single bullet had cut through on his right side, missing other neatly-packed vital organs. Barring any serious infection, his early prognosis looked good. I leaned my head back and flicked my eyes heavenward.

My next call was to the District 9 station. When I identified myself, the desk sergeant sounded like an old buddy. Kill a cop-killer and you get all the love. He told me that Jerri Hanady had been released on bond, and that Miss Brennan was still being held. That meant she wasn't talking. Had to hand it to her. Even though her boss no longer had a care in the world, she was still protecting him. Or maybe just herself.

Next, I planned my call to Jerri Hanady. It wouldn't be easy to talk with a client who just killed her husband. Maybe I'd better do it from the office. I showered, shaved, and changed my clothes. I felt like a new man, born again somehow, from the detritus of death.

I arrived in the industrial court at about 9:30. It was bright out, but the sunshine didn't seem so punishing. The kids were playing in the fenced yard next to the preschool. I watched them for a full minute before going inside my office. When this was all over, I would pay a personal visit to Marni Reyes, too.

Inside my office, I just stood there, staring with unfocused eyes at my desk. For the life of me, I couldn't remember why I had decided to go there. The phone. Right. Ella, the Hanady's cook, answered after six rings. She spoke in a hushed tone.

"Miss Ella," I said, "this is Ed Darvis."

Before I could ask to speak to Mrs. Hanady, Ella said, "She sleepin', Mr. Dahvis."

"That's good. Don't wake her on my account. I'll be in my office all afternoon. She can reach me later."

"I'll be sure to tell her you called."

I hung up, leaned back in my chair, and put my feet up on my desk to wait—and think. Again, my thoughts turned to Meeki. He'd mentioned investors in Colombia. I pictured fat, rich, bald Americans getting heavy on young field workers. Were the girls just used for sex? No, they were impregnated, too. Baby-making machines. I snorted as I wondered if they were seeded according to some sick design. I wondered how many other adoptions had gone through besides Rachel's. I shook off more questions. All this was just too much to take in. And, with weird relief, I figured it was a federal issue now. Extradition. Grand Juries. I would have to testify in Jerri Hanady's trial. That I knew. She wasn't gas chamber material, but if she was lucky, she'd get manslaughter and ten years. Maybe a partially suspended sentence. And, of course, there was her daughter to consider. For a brief time inside Miss Brennan's bungalow, I wondered if Meeki had molested her. I didn't have the luxury of contemplating her health in such a tense scene, but now thoughts of the giant petting her, or doing worse, filled my head. I shook my head to banish my thoughts about the little girl. This is a hell of a way to make a living for a couple day's work. Then it hit me. If I even got fucking paid.

I stood up and looked outside as some of the leaves on the Bradford Pears rocked back and forth in the breeze. Tomorrow I'd try to get in to see Bertie. That bullet he took could have been for me. We were even now. A bullet for each other. A bullet apiece. But then, I was just counting for the hell of it, because friends never owe.

In a couple of hours the afternoon pickup would begin across the street. Maybe I'd cut across after that and find Marni Reyes. Maybe I'd just leave her the hell alone.

In the meantime, I decided to ignore everything else I should be doing. I owed it to myself. I lit a cigarette, sat down, and propped my feet back up on the desk. As the pear trees swayed, the image of Meeki Osagae's dead face seemed to materialize amid their black boughs. I shuddered to shake the vision.

I woke up with a start, my shirtfront soaking wet.

Stiff, I pulled myself up and stretched as I walked over to the counter and put some coffee on to brew. Then I lit another cigarette. Then I stubbed it out.

I picked up a crushed butt off the linoleum.

I sorted through some bills on my desktop.

I put my feet back up on the desk and thought about my life.

Tired of everything—my routine, the shitty hands I kept getting dealt, my job, my life, myself, I picked up the phone. The business with Broad Jimmy—and my being an accomplice in hiding a murder—still had to be dealt with. Maybe he'd want to decline my services at this point. That would be A-OK. Hell, at this point, I wanted him to.

I called my answering service. I had two messages. I

could tell by the eager tone in the messenger's voice—that brief note that masked the ever-funny 'yuck, yuck, yuck' I imagined she'd shared with her fellow messengers—that she'd been looking forward to this call.

"The first is from a man named Jimmy."

"Yeah."

"He said, um, do you want me to quote, or just paraphrase?"

"Is it quotable?"

She snickered. "Well, yes … and no. There's some language.…"

"I can take it, if you can, honey."

"Here goes, then. But don't say I didn't warn you." At this she laughed. "He said, 'Darvis, you dick-smoking PI, where the hell are you?'" I heard giggles in the background. Her sidekicks most likely listening in. "'Pull your pud out of your light socket, comb your hair back down, and get your flabby ass down to my place. Pronto'. Then he spelled out the word 'pronto'. Shall I spell it out for you, too?" Without waiting, she started, "P-R-O—."

"I think I got it. Anything more?"

"No." She sounded disappointed by my lack of reaction. She added, "Isn't that enough?!" Her full-throated laugh, followed by some harsh shushing, set me on edge. "But I do think he may have tried to pick me up. He sounded a little bit in his cups."

"He's like that. And the other message?"

Again, she laughed. "She didn't leave her name, but she wanted me to ask if you needed your…and I quote—'venetian blinds cleaned?'—unquote."

This time, I laughed right along with her. "Boy, do I. But maybe another time, hon. And thanks."

Back home I twisted open the lock to my mailbox in the building foyer and pulled out a stack of more bills. Nothing there that couldn't wait a few days. Also nothing to help delay me thinking about The Beef's murder. I retired upstairs to my wingback chair, loosened my collar, and kicked off my loafers. If I wasn't careful, I'd fall asleep, but the uncomfortable chair worked against that. My stomach growled, but I didn't know whether to feed it breakfast or lunch. Think Darvis. Think. You light socket-fucking idiot, you.

Officer Downing's nightstick still lay on the side table. He may not have slit The Beef's throat, but he was involved. I just wasn't sure exactly how. At least not yet. I had called The Beef's death a vengeance killing. I didn't know his death from a common mugging, yet Downing didn't correct my identification of the crime. You get matter-of-fact with people and push their buttons, and eventually they'll trap themselves in their own defense mechanisms. This I knew. Experience paid for something.

I check-listed what I knew so far. Someone had it in for George Reynolds. Based on the way he treated folks, more than a few people did. Tim Hamill, the cabbie, who had implied he spoke to Kira Harto on the phone the night The Beef was murdered, but said he didn't recognize her voice. Yet, when she called the cab company, she would have gotten a dispatcher, not Hamill. Either he was sloppy about his lies, or she hadn't gone through the dispatcher at all. Which, in that case, meant she called Hamill directly. And she was involved.

But why? The fact that Hamill lived in Dogtown, part of Officer Downing's beat, was a little too convenient. They could be accomplices. Also, Hamill claimed not to know or recognize Kira Harto at the bar. Something was fouling the gears of a plan, and Hamill was the grime. He covered the most territory in this situation. Plus, he spilled too easily. Let's say, I told myself, an arrangement had been made to off The Beef in the alley next to Broad Jimmy's. Kira could have called the killer after everyone else had left the bar and while The Beef was relieving himself outside. She also could have reached Hamill to arrange for a pickup, which would also have given him an alibi: drunk guy at a bar at the end of the night gets cab ride. That guaranteed that Hamill was a witness, if not an accomplice. In this scenario, Kira was deeply involved. If so, why? And was Broad Jimmy involved, too? I thought back to his demeanor and appearance last night. He looked like he had been asleep. His defenses were down, and some nervousness was playing around his tough edges. Was it the nervousness? Or involvement? Or could his demeanor be chalked up to having a regular customer killed outside of his establishment? Even more sinister, could Kira be involved in something as complicated as murder right under Broad Jimmy's nose?

I didn't know if Jimmy and Kira would be awake yet, but I needed to talk to them before I went any further. I picked up a contract to give to Broad Jimmy, swallowed down some cold, burned black coffee, and walked out the front door. As I closed it, I tucked a flyer advertising a cleaning service into the doorframe underneath the bottom hinge. Then I locked the door. If anyone decided to make any surprise visits while I was gone, I'd know.

I drove east on Route 40 and made Locust in about ten minutes. My watch said quarter to twelve. One of the two unlikely love birds would be awake by now, getting ready for the liquid lunch special the salesmen and stock brokers traded on.

I parked at a meter and fed it its thirty pieces. Broad Jimmy's looked dark inside. I tried the door, but it was locked. I stepped back to take in a fuller view of the place. There wasn't much foot traffic at this end of downtown. I noticed a little sign taped up to the left of the front door. In a quick-looking neat hand, it read:

Closed due to illness. Expect to be open again tonight.

Well, I didn't blame them. I doubted Jimmy would be able to keep his cool—or keep from spilling what happened to someone. Kira would be able to, though. Ching-chong crap, as Jimmy said. What other secrets do you possess, Kira?

I walked around to the alley and saw it for the first time in daylight. There were the usual metal trashcans and a dumpster. Kira and Jimmy kept it remarkably clean. There was an extra level of dazzle, thanks to Kira's wash job last night. Or maybe she just shined up the grime. The untrained eye wouldn't notice anything.

A fire escape climbed the brick wall near the dumpster. The retractable ladder leading up to the stairs was halfway down. I jumped a few times and finally caught hold of the bottom rung. It slid down, the clatter of squeaky iron echoing in the alley. I started up, huffing and puffing when I reached the landing. Maybe I needed to cut down on the smokes. On the second floor there was a dark window. I pushed my face up to the glass. An un-curtained bathroom. Guess you don't need much privacy with another brick wall for a neighbor. I continued to climb to the top floor to another window. This one looked into a bedroom. No curtain here, either. The place had a light clutter of discarded crumpled paper and file boxes. A twin bed was pushed against the right wall. Broad Jimmy's sleeping form filled it. He was wearing a tanktop t-shirt and boxers. The yellow robe lay crumpled on the floor. One of his tattooed arms, the one with the squashed Japanese soldier on it, lay across his face. His body and the general disorder of the room belied the definite lack of a feminine touch. So, Jimmy and Kira slept in separate rooms. The door to the bedroom was closed. I couldn't hear any sounds coming from the apartment.

I climbed back down the fire escape and gave the ladder a good push to get it back up. It grated to a stop halfway. I'd leave it how it was then. I stood in the alley, right over the spot were The Beef's body had lain. Jimmy was sacked out. No visible sign of Kira Harto. The tavern was closed. This all felt funny. Something wasn't right.

I got back into the Chevy and decided to go by St. Mary's to see if I could visit Bertie. Later, I could try to find the cab dispatcher, Ben Hartog, in the phone book and talk to him face to face. Not that I had high hopes of him being overly cooperative, though.

15. BACK INTO THE LION'S DEN

When I came in the hospital room door, Bertie raised a coffee mug.

"Whatcha got in there, Bertie?"

"It's just water, detective. But cheers anyway."

"Don't tell me you're off duty because of a little scratch?"

"Naw. It's just my lunch hour." He gestured at a plastic chair. "Have a seat. Miss Weathersby, is it? Now, I'll be the one to ask the questions." Bertie giggled, of all things. "Tell me about your estranged husband and why you think he's dead." I smiled at that, then sat in the flimsy chair. Bertie must have a dandy narcotic on board. He looked strangely relaxed, while I was feeling sleepless and uncomfortable.

"You look like shit, Ed. Broad Jimmy's already treat you right today?" It was my turn to stiffen. I passed off the sudden jolt with a big yawn.

"You know me. Never met a happy hour that didn't deliver. How are you feeling?"

He shrugged and gestured impassively at his abdomen. Bertie was too casual. His left hand trembled almost imperceptibly.

"Yeah, well. I wanted to see if you wanted a Hi-Lo rematch. So I could take back some of my money."

"You're on. Got the cards?"

I nodded, took out the pack, and handed it to him. I lit a cigarette, too, which drew a look from Bertie.

"Feel strange to be in here, Ed?"

"I'll say. Especially with the likes of your mug looking at me."

"The view ain't so pretty from over here, either."

"I'll give you that." He shuffled the deck on his tray and I cut the cards. He started to deal as I blew out a smoke ring. When he winced, I stayed his hand, then took the deck away from him. He lay back and blew a breath out slowly. I dealt instead.

"Bertie," He seemed to know what I was going to say.

"Ed, don't bother. I'll be all right."

I wanted to reassure him, ask him how he felt, make sure the pain wasn't too bad. I also wanted to fish for any mention of The Beef's disappearance. I wanted to insure he knew nothing about The Beef, or worse, my involvement in hiding his body. Actually, I didn't want to hear anything about The Beef coming from Bertie's lips.

"You know George 'The Beef' Reynolds?"

Damn. I leaned over to fiddle with one of my shoes, keeping my eyes averted.

"Sure. I wouldn't call him a pal, but I know him. He holds court at Broad Jimmy's most nights. You can get a ringside seat every night if you want. Some lucky customers even get a chance to fight him."

"Including you?"

I raised up and steeled myself. "Nix. The Beef may be retired, but I wouldn't put him on my dance card." I paused to pull on the cigarette. I squinted as I did so, but my eyes were riveted on his face, scanning for a tell. "Why do you ask?"

"Some buddies of mine in the Three are looking for him."

"Oh, yeah?"

Bertie just studied me. I studied the face-up cards as though I was unsure of my next move. "Where'd he go?" I asked, without looking him in the eye.

"They don't know. But he's in some shit."

And how, I thought. Frozen shit.

"What'd he do?"

"He's been rigging fights on the South side. Amateur stuff. But he's suspected in some backroom deals. Illegal gambling."

"Small stuff. And common. Why the sudden interest in bringing him in?"

"There's been some talk. Possible mob connection. Maybe a hit or two. That gets the local boys worked up. Might mean Feds."

I forced a chuckle. "Territorial pissing."

"You got it. It's bad enough having to deal with you PI's." He smiled emptily at me and turned over a queen of diamonds. We played for about half an hour. I barely spoke, but Bertie held up his end of the conversation cheerfully. Neither of us was addressing the previous night's events. I had more than Meeki's killing on my mind. I was feeling guilty. I wanted to spill what I was involved in and solicit his help. I was close to opening up a few times, but I couldn't get past the feeling of The Beef's dead weight in my arms as Broad Jimmy and I slung him into the basement freezer. Until I put together a few more pieces, I would have to keep my lips sealed around Bertie. And that hurt in a way. To my knowledge, he had always dealt straight with me. I couldn't think of a more honest guy.

In fact, it reminded me of the time I was having girl trouble at sixteen. My father was off philandering on a sales trip somewhere. My mother was sweet with me, but her advice about love was old-fashioned: you wait until you're married, and that's that. The problem, as it was, was that I finally got with this hot number who put out once, but then strung me along, holding back after that. I was convinced I was in love with her and something was wrong with me because she wouldn't let me touch her. I recriminated myself, tried to do anything to please her, even wrote her love letters. But no soap. Every night I lay awake, sleepless, anxious, horny. Even afraid. How could I tell my mother that my sanity depended on getting some? My mother could tell something was eating at me, but there was no way I could talk about sex with her. Eventually, this girl and I hit the sheets again; I don't know to this day what made her change her mind. We lasted maybe another two months. My mother was relieved when it was over. I was, too, but for reasons I could never tell her about. I never learned what—or if—I did wrong. Since then, I haven't gotten close enough to anyone for long enough to feel much more than a strong lust. And with my few friends, I was just as cautious. I couldn't open up to Bertie.

Around 1:30, a dour nurse poked her head in, frowning at me and my smoke, before curtly announcing the end of visiting hours. I left the cards for Bertie, then paused at the door longer than usual when I said goodbye. Bertie's composure made me nervous. Like my mother, he could tell something was eating at me, but he didn't pry.

When I got back to the office, I looked up Ben Hartog from Yellow Cab in the phone book. He was listed as having a South City address, near Holly Hills. If it had been Dogtown, I'd have wet my pants. I called his number and let it ring. At last someone picked up.

"Yeah?" A sleepy voice.

"This Ben Hartog?"

"Yeah. What is it?"

I contemplated beginning my calls with offers of free sweepstakes tickets after today.

"This is Ed Darvis. I'm a private investigator."

"What can I do for you, Mr. Darvis?" Now there was a change. Either this guy was polite, or he had something to hide.

"I'm investigating a case that involves one of your drivers. He may have been witness to a petty crime, but this crime involves a VIP. You know how that is. I can't really say much more."

"Yeah, I understand. Uh, what can I do to help?"

"Were you working the late shift two nights ago?"

"I was."

"Did you get any calls from foreigners? Oriental-sound-ing voice?"

"Let me think," he said. A few seconds ticked by. "Yeah, there was one. German voice, though. Male. That work?"

"Not quite. Any others? A woman's voice maybe?"

"Nope. Just the one German. I'd have remembered a woman's voice. Oriental, you say? Especially that. I can't understand what they're saying half the time. Mr. Ferris, he manages our garage, he wanted to give dispatcher duty to this Jap driver. A guy from California. Ferris thinks his English is good enough. Can you imagine? He says 'derivery'! No one can understand him. I mean—"

Irritated, I cut him off. "I get you. Listen. Anybody ever call cabbies directly? You know, have a favorite, and bypass dispatch?"

"Not that I know of. And Mr. Ferris would be pissed off to hear about it. We gotta log all our drivers' hours and routes. There's no pickup we don't know about."

"Okay, Mr. Hartog. You've been very helpful. Thanks."

"Hey, don't mention it." He sounded like I had made his day. If that was the case, I felt sad for him. I hung up the phone and pressed my fingers to my lips. Unconsciously, I brought my index and middle fingers together as though I had a cigarette. A thought was about to break to the surface of my mind, but it would need a little nicotine enticement. I lit a cigarette and got up to pace in front of my desk. A few dust bunnies got wise and scattered.

Okay, the dispatcher said he didn't get a call from a woman, so, let's say Kira called the cabbie directly. Maybe they had a deal. She'd call him to pick up the drunks, he'd collect the fare, and split the profits with her. That would make sense. Hell, maybe they even had a deal where Hamill would rifle their pockets and split that kitty with her as well. Only one problem. Hamill claimed he didn't recognize Kira. And he thought he might even stand to get robbed going to Broad Jimmy's at that hour. So that didn't fit.

I thought about the Closed sign outside the tavern. I pictured Broad Jimmy's sleeping form in the closed-up room. That's what made it click. I've been sweating all day. Jimmy was asleep in a sealed room with no fan. In this heat, a third-floor room of a brick building, downtown, would be hotter than a kiln. But I couldn't see any sweat in my mind's eye. His body had looked hairy, yeah, but dry.

The funny feeling I'd had outside the tavern returned, this time intensified. I jumped up, locked my office door, and got in the Chevy. The humidity punished me immediately, and until I got on Route 40 East, I cursed the sluggish traffic. Once on the highway, I opened her up. I made Locust faster than ever and parked at a meter without giving a thought to satisfying it. The sign in front of Broad

Jimmy's was gone. I got out and tried the tavern's door. It opened. Inside, the usual low lights were on, the dirty ceiling swathed in gloom. A couple of suits were engaged in one-upmanship at a table in the center of the room, their faces red with laughter and drink. A few other singletons hunched over tables. A glance behind the bar showed me Kira Harto's back, clad in regulation tight black. I walked up to the bar and sat on a stool. She turned around with two dripping shot glasses in her hands.

"Hey, soldier. You here earlier than usual. What you have?" She had raised her voice to say this, so no one would suspect anything unusual.

I looked deep into her eyes. She didn't betray anything but a casual acquaintance with me. I pulled out a cigarette and looked around at the two drunken businessmen on the other side of the pool table. One laughed loudly, and the other gripped the tabletop. They were lost in their own bluster. I looked back at Kira and spoke in a low voice.

"Where's Jimmy?"

"He sleeping. He got to work late tonight," she answered, in the same loud tone.

"Cut the act, Kira."

She glared at me over her tight smile. Leaning close she whispered, "Fuck you. And like it." She stepped back and picked up the shot glasses. Without taking her eyes off me, she started drying them.

I blew smoke in her face. She wrinkled her delicate nose, but she didn't say anything.

"I wanna see him."

"Who?" she asked stupidly, and sarcastically.

I remembered the contract. "I've got that contract for Jimmy to sign. How about I just go up and slip it under his door?"

"I'm perfectly capable of bringing a slip of paper to my husband," she muttered.

"I know you are, Kira. That and more, I'm sure. I just feel better putting the paper in my client's hands. You know."

"That's as good as saying you don't trust me," she returned.

"Not at all. Just one of the few formalities of my job I let myself enjoy."

"Well, you can give it to me, or wait until tonight. He's sleeping. He's not feeling well."

"I understand. The Beef was a heavy lug."

She shoved her drying towel forcefully into one of the glasses. I just sat there and watched her for a moment, taking long drags and blowing the smoke out slowly.

"Okay, Kira. I'll come back tonight. Say, your bathroom working at this hour?"

"Why wouldn't it be?" she said in a harsh stage whisper. The two businessmen were oblivious. I smiled at her, stubbed out my cigarette, and returned the contract to my inside coat pocket. I went towards the john, taking my time opening the door. I looked back in her direction, but she had turned around to grab some more soapy glasses. It's now or never, I thought.

I ducked down out of her line of sight and scurried along the back wall away from the bathroom door and towards the far end of the bar. Kira's back was still turned. I scooted under the hinged bar top that separated the bar back from the main room, and slipped between the curtains to the kitchen. I'd only been back here once before. The body in my arms had distracted me from the décor. Yeah, a dead body would do that. The usual white pickle buckets, silverware, and metal drying racks greeted me. I waited just inside the curtain for a couple of seconds to see if Kira had noticed me. Luck struck for the second time today. That gave me one more bout of it for later. I had a feeling I'd need it. Good things aren't the only things that come in threes.

I knew I'd have to act fast. I found a door at the rear of the kitchen and pulled it open. A flight of stairs led up to the second floor. I took the steps two at a time and came to a landing with another door. It was locked. So, I hurried up the next flight and found a door there open. But I had to stop. In between ragged breaths, I cursed the stifling heat and my lack of endurance in taking the two sets of stairs in record time.

When I walked through the doorway, it was like an intersection leading to three different rooms. I peeked into the room on the right, which led to a small kitchen. I walked over to the next one. It led to a living room. A quick calculation told me that the door on the left was Jimmy's room, the one I'd seen earlier from the fire escape. I knocked loudly on the door a couple of times, then waited. No sound. Nothing. I turned the knob and eased the door open. The stifling, stale heat overwhelmed me. Across the room was the window that led to the fire escape. To my left was Broad Jimmy's bed. He was still there, lying in the exact same position I had seen this morning. I didn't waste time with speculation, but reached for his wrist and felt for a pulse. There was one. A very weak one. Maybe because I knew his blood had slowed, his body temperature seemed cooler than the air. This wasn't the first time I'd seen a drugged man. Must have taken horse tranquilizers to keep him down this long. I thought about what to do. One thing for sure, I had to get some air into this room. It felt like an attic in summer, which is basically what it was at the moment. I walked to the window and opened it. Funny when summer humidity is a welcome respite. I let the air run through the window a minute. I knew Kira would start wondering what I was doing for so long in the John. And I wouldn't put it past her to pry open the men's room door, or have one of the business lushes go in after me. I walked over and closed the door to Jimmy's room. Then I stepped over the sill and onto the fire escape. I thought about closing the window, but I worried about Jimmy. He could die in there in his state. I left the window up and descended the stairs. The retractable ladder gave up from its stuck position with some more sweat on my part. I jumped down to the alley and left the ladder down this time. I realized I was leaving Kira a trail, but right then, I didn't care. Just call it returning the 'fuck you'.

I got back in the Chevy and drove away from the tavern and back onto Locust. I decided to skip my office for the time being and get something to eat at home. Tonight would be busy.

16. A MISSING PACKAGE

I came up the back stairs of my building and walked down my hallway. The cleaning service flyer was still stuck in the doorframe where I had left it. Even so, I unlocked my door and pushed it all the way open before entering. The apartment was airy with its windows open after trudging along the stuffy hallway. I pulled out my .38 and held it at arms length in front of me. I swung the gun behind the door and looked before I moved on. Out of obsessive practice, or maybe it was the unwavering prickling along my neck and back, I investigated each room—the front room, the hallway, my bedroom, and part of the kitchen. Not a sign of anyone. Nothing out of place. But that feeling kept cropping up. Finally, convinced I was just wrung out and nervous from the odd scene at Broad Jimmy's, I sighed and went into the kitchen. Another pressed-meat sandwich and a cold beer later, I felt like I could sleep. I sat down in the armchair in the front room and laid the .38 on the end table. I put my feet up on my hassock and faced the door. If anyone decided to try me, I'd at least have a sporting chance. With that, I fell into unconsciousness.

I woke up with the late-afternoon light, and with a nice

quantity of drool down my chin and my shirtfront. My neck ached from the odd angle with which it rested against the back of the chair. I stood up, tasting stale cigarettes, and burped pressed meat. The only thing to chase the twin tastes was a fresh cigarette and a strong drink. I had both, then undressed and showered. I shaved carefully and got dressed. My kitchen wall clock said six-forty. I'd slept longer than I planned to, but my body knew what I needed, and I was grateful. Besides, what difference did it make? If my body believed it was a new day, maybe it would go to work on my mind, too.

I walked out of my apartment, put the cleaning service flyer back in the crack, and locked up. Between my recent shower, the humidity in my apartment, and the closeness of heat in the hallway, sweat broke across my forehead. I flashed back to Jimmy lying unconscious in his room. I started to worry that maybe just leaving his window open hadn't been enough. Maybe I should have splashed some water on him and then run like hell. I couldn't risk calling for an ambulance, which might bring police. And if they came and put the screws to Kira, I wouldn't put it past her to finger me for involvement in The Beef's slaying, or subsequent handling. No, I had to leave Jimmy. But it felt rotten.

I got to the garage and started up the Chevy. Traffic was tied up on the surface streets, and rolling down my windows just let the swelter in, but once I made Route 40, it was clear, and I got a hot breeze to dry my face. Suckers on the other side were parked in the jam, heading away from downtown. I pulled off on Jefferson and connected with Locust. I could do this route on autopilot now.

I parked out of sight at Broad Jimmy's. I didn't want my car to be spotted, although I couldn't say why. I walked up around the other side of the block and drew near the alley. The fire escape ladder was still down as I had left it. Looking up, I saw that Jimmy's bedroom window was closed. I looked at my watch: 7:18. Jimmy's would be hopping now, with the happy hour crowd gone full bore—which was a good time to mingle and see what was up.

I walked through the door. The place was awash in smoke, the clink of glasses, and the seagull chatter of happy drunks. Kira was behind the bar, smiling demurely at some sap. At the end of the bar, where The Beef had lorded it over his audience yesterday, only one man sat. Simple Simon.

I walked along the bar, dodging elbows, and the totter of a gesturing businessman. I looked Kira's way and gave her a tight-lipped smile. Her expression barely changed when she saw me. I went straight to Simple Simon's side. His usual nervousness reached a peak when I sat down next to him.

"What's new, Simon old buddy? How was work today?"

Simon stiffened and gave me a fatigued, edgy look. His grey beard looked more ashen than his face. A few stray hairs jutted out from his jaw and towards his neck, like desperate saplings losing purchase on an eroding slope.

"What do you want?" he muttered.

"Simon, you gettin' tough on me? The Beef ain't here now." I wanted him even edgier, to put the press on. "I'm surprised you got your back to the door."

He turned on his stool and eyed the front door, and then looked back at me. "What do you mean?" Simon jumped when a glass shattered and cries of delight, as well as pity, swelled over the seagull chatter.

"You got good reflexes. You're not half-crocked yet."

"Why don't you mind your own business?" He glared at me, his face turning hard. That surprised me. The Beef was less than twenty-four hours dead and Simon was already looking to step into his spats.

"That's what I'm doing, Simon." I left it at that. I stood up, clapped him on the back, and walked toward the other end of the bar. I got some of the same jostles going back from the business yegs. The place was packed, and no one seemed the wiser that a crime had been committed here not twenty-four hours before. I took a seat at the corner of the bar—where I could see the door—and lit up a cigarette. Kira Harto was still playing the coquette. I watched her work for a few minutes, impressed with her act. Every now and again I heard her voice over the hubbub. "You no say?" "You go on, big guy!" "Hi, soldier, what you have?" I felt an impulse to clutch her neck and squeeze, but it passed. At last she walked over to me. She stood in front of me, but she wasn't looking at me. She mumbled something.

"I didn't quite catch that, Kira hon," I said.

She leaned over the bar. "I said 'Go away'." She gritted her teeth.

"I said I'd be back later. You know. With the contract." I patted my coat pocket, but didn't smile.

"Jimmy's asleep."

I leaned in near her neck. "We know that's a lie," I whispered harshly. "Now, go get him."

"What if I don't?" she returned, just as hard.

"Then I'll just invite Officer Downing over for a few drinks on me." She stiffened, then looked down. "Yeah, that's right. He paid me a little visit. And he wasn't exactly happy to be fingered as The Beef's assassin."

She looked up at me finally. Someone sitting at the middle of the bar called out, "Where's that Bud, baby? Man's thirsty." Jesus, it was my Uncle Charles. I motioned for her to go serve him; I picked up a copy of the Globe-Democrat, half wet with beer, and pretended to be interested in what I was looking at. When I looked around a minute later, my uncle had joined a group of other blue-collar guys near the pool table. Kira had gone to the far end of the bar, near Simple Simon—and the kitchen entrance. She was turned in profile to him but her back was to me, so I couldn't tell if she was communicating anything to him. But he looked up at her in all the noise and then shot a look down at me. After that he stood up and made his way to the front door. I got up and intercepted him, blocking his exit.

"Stay away from me," he hissed.

"Where you going so fast, Simon? I was just about to order a round for the both of us."

"Get the fuck out of my way."

When he sidestepped me, I grabbed his right arm, exactly where the nerve near his elbow was and squeezed.

"God . . . damn!" he yelled as he started to sag toward the floor. A guy seated near me looked up and said, "Hey." I ignored him and looked back towards the kitchen. Broad Jimmy stood in the doorway, still wearing a tank-top, the bottom hanging loosely from his belly and over a pair of dark slacks. He looked like he'd been run over, propped up, and bull-whipped. I let go of Simon.

"N-next time I'll cut you, you bastard," he said as he ran out the door. Fat chance, I thought.

I pushed through the crowd toward Jimmy, making sure to stay close to the bar, and away from my uncle. Fortunately, he didn't see me. My eyes locked on Broad Jimmy's. He mouthed the word "You" and gestured for me to come over. When I got to the hinged bar top, he leaned toward me and said, "We've got a big fuckin' problem." He turned and headed back into the kitchen. I lifted the bar top and followed.

We were alone. In the fluorescent light of the kitchen, he looked like a ghost. His eyes were red-rimmed, and stubble stood out on his jaw.

"Follow me, Darvis."

I did as I was told.

We walked past the door that led upstairs, toward another door. The one that descended to the basement. Not particularly fond of following him downstairs, I got nervous something was up. Jimmy opened the door and started down the stairs. If he had something in store for me, at least I was above and behind him. I could use my feet to kick him down the stairs, and then turn and bound up the stairs, if needed. He reached the bottom without turning around and strode through the dampness straight toward the freezer. A chill ran over me, despite the heat and humidity.

Jimmy opened the door to the freezer and growled, "Look."

Although I wasn't particularly fond of looking at the cold dead body of The Beef, I leaned over and looked into the freezer and then back at Jimmy. In any other situation it would sound funny or trivial: The Beef is missing from the freezer. This sight was neither of the above. "What'd you do with him?"

"What'd I do with him?" He grabbed my lapels. "Not a goddamn thing! I wanted to ask you the same damn thing!"

"Don't be stupid. Why would I take him out of here?"

Enraged, Jimmy shoved me against a freezer rack. "Then where the fuck is the body?" I kept my hands at my side in a play for docility. "Kira said you were nosing around this morning. She said you pulled a fast one on her and left. Then after you left, she checked the freezer and The Beef's body was gone." He clutched my lapels closer together and squeezed, his knuckles pressing into my windpipe. His red-rimmed eyes bulged from his giant face. I thought how easy it would be for him to lay me out right there, put me in The Beef's place.

"Jimmy," I managed to squawk, "Jimmy, I can't breathe. Gimme some air."

"I'll give you some air," he snarled. "James Cagney style!" The thought of another bullet in me didn't make me jump for joy, not that I could dream of doing that while in Jimmy's hard grasp.

He pulled back his knuckles, but kept my lapels roughly bunched. "Look, I did give Kira the slip. But I didn't come down here. I swear to you. I went upstairs. For Godsakes, let up a little, Jimmy." He stood there a moment and then released my lapels altogether when it registered I'd gone upstairs, not down. But he didn't move from in front of me. I would have been just as comfortable in an iron maiden open just a crack.

"Start talking."

"I brought the contract by, for you to sign. You know, for my services. Kira said you were sleeping. I didn't believe her. So, I told her I'd just slip the contract under your door, but she said no dice. And since you were still supposedly sleeping since I'd seen you this morning, I had a funny feeling. When her back was turned, I snuck through the kitchen door and went up the stairs."

Jimmy slammed his hand against the shelf behind my head. Something toppled off and struck me. I winced, but held still.

"I found your room. Jimmy, you were laying in the same position I saw you in earlier.

"Earlier?"

"Yeah, I'd climbed up the fire escape ladder and peeked

in on you. I thought you were just sleeping then. The room was closed up. You were breathing all shallow. I got worried and left a window open. Then. . . ," I let out a breath and breathed in the frigid air deeply, "I took the fire escape back down. That was it. I don't know anything about The Beef."

"Why didn't you listen to Kira, hunh? My wife, you bastard. You don't come into my house. You don't ignore her. I ought to beat the shit out of you."

"Save it, Jimmy. Save it for whoever is behind all this."

"I can't think. It's too fuckin' cold in here! Get out of the way." He shoved past me and began pacing the small space outside the freezer. I straightened my shirt and adjusted my jacket. I didn't say anything for a full minute, while Jimmy paced and scowled.

"Jimmy. Simple Simon was just in here. When I came in and sat down beside him, he was all hinky. And he left in a big hurry. I think his story doesn't wash."

"What story is that?"

"He said he left the bar before The Beef. A good half-hour before he did. He swears he took a bus home. I'm starting not to believe him. I think he's involved in The Beef's death."

"That little pipsqueak? That … that pussy?"

"Why not? He was terrified of The Beef. He made it seem like he was entertained by him. But he wasn't. Maybe his fear, the humiliation The Beef thrust on him, turned into anger. Maybe he wanted to see The Beef hurt, humiliated. Maybe even dead. Simon's got motive running out of his ass."

Jimmy stopped pacing for a moment. He smiled a sick smile. "Well, what are you waiting for, dick? Bring him in to me."

I stood regarding him. He looked dead serious, murderous.

I unbuttoned my jacket.

"Am I still in your employ then?"

"You got that right."

I withdrew the contract from my pocket and passed it to Jimmy.

Jimmy let me out a side door from the kitchen and into the now-infamous alley. I wanted to talk to Kira desperately, but with the crowd and her attitude toward me, I knew I wouldn't get far. So, I took the alley and strode over The Beef's murder spot. I walked up the block and got into my car. Should I go straight to Simon's? Probably. I didn't expect to find him, though.

I got off Route 40 at Hampton Avenue and zigzagged around the narrow one-way Dogtown streets to Nashville. I parked at the top of the block, several houses east of Simon's bungalow. The late evening sun was out of my eyes as I descended to Simon's house. As the bright after-image cleared from my eyes, a few kids playing stickball materialized in the street. Someone was barbecuing. I flashed back to my own block when I was a kid in north St. Louis. We lived across from a meat-processing plant with a butcher's in front. My old man would go over evenings and sweet-talk turkey necks and gizzards out of the proprietor for stew. Maybe a taste or two with the guy, which often led to a drinking bout, and gambling the dole, or some scrounged cash. My sister and I would watch for him to come back, both our stomachs growling, her falling asleep on the couch most of the time. Yeah, those were the days.

Simon's house sat on the north side of Nashville. I decided to case it before I knocked on the door. Facing the house, I took the breezeway on the right side of the house, my eyes on the windows. All were covered with shades. In back, a neglected yard gave up trying to grow anything before succumbing to a dilapidated garage. A rusted chain-link fence stretched to meet it. I stepped up onto the small back porch and peered into the back door window. Simon's kitchen. It was empty, save for a sink full of dishes and a small Formica table. The hallway leaving the kitchen bent at an angle, so I couldn't see any further. I could see the other side of the house, which was blocked by the chain-link fence, no gate. I creaked down the rotten porch steps and went around to that side. Just as I was about to hike a leg over the fence, I heard the motor of a car as it ran past the house, heading east, and then the sudden squeal of bad brakes. I ducked down and hurried around to the back of the house, and started back up the breezeway. But as I edged along the brick wall of Simon's house, I heard a car door slam. I froze for a minute, listening. Then, I risked a look around an untrimmed yew.

There, standing in the middle of the street on the driver's side of a cab, was Simon, leaning over talking to the cabbie. His blue work shirt was soaked with sweat around his armpits and lower back. As he straightened, he slapped the top of the cab lightly, and turned to walk to his front sidewalk as the cab took off. I ducked back down behind the bush and waited for the cab to pull up the street. And what do you know. Tim Hamill was behind the wheel.

I waited until I heard Simon's footsteps on the cement steps, then I hunched over and skirted alongside the house to the front. Keeping low, I snuck along the unkempt yews to the front door. Then, just as Simon turned the key in his lock and opened the door, I bolted onto the porch, grabbed him, and shoved him inside. He fell to the carpet and I slammed the door all in one motion.

Simon rolled over and looked up at me. "You! You get away from me. I'm calling the cops."

"Good idea," I said. "Ask for Officer Downing."

He turned pale. "What's that supposed to mean?"

I ignored his question. "Simon, you were in an awful hurry to get out of Broad Jimmy's. What gives?"

"Nothin' to do with you, creep. Now get out."

I took two steps forward and used one leg to put pressure on Simon's ankle. He howled.

"Gah—get off me!"

"Not till you answer some questions and cut the bullshit."

"Fuck you!" He spat up at me. I applied more pressure to his ankle and he screamed out. I didn't want to play it this way, but Simon needed to *feel* that I was in charge, not just know it. Even so, there were plenty of people outside. Someone might hear him howling and wonder what the hell was going on. So, I eased my foot up from his ankle. Just enough to stop his screams. The man was near tears. I looked down at his receding chin and graying beard. At once, I felt like a cheap hood.

But this was no time to get soft. "What were you doin' hookin' a ride with Tim Hamill? Hunh?"

"What?" he cried out. "Since when does a man have to justify a cab ride?" Simon attempted to sit up, but immediately fell back as I again applied more pressure to his ankle. He groaned and wiped at his eyes quickly with the back of one arm.

"If I let up on you, will you talk? Straight?"

After a minute, he nodded. I removed my foot and stepped back, but stood ready to attack him, if need be. He turned over and crawled away from me over to the loveseat like a dog. As he rose up and turned to sit down, he flung something at me. I had just enough time to register the flash of steel before the knife struck my right kneecap and glanced off, and I fell on my back to the floor, pierced with pain. In an instant, Simon leapt off the couch and straddled me. At first, he went for my throat, but then he clawed at my face. He did everything but punch me. And that was his crucial mistake.

Ignoring my pain, I grabbed the fingers of one of his hands and bent them backwards until he yelled and fell sideways, trying to escape me. That gave me just enough leeway to push him off of me. Still holding onto his hand, I pulled myself up on my knees. Only then did I let go of his hand. Then, ignoring restraint, I hammered relentlessly at his face with both fists. Within moments, Simon was slumped on the floor, blood oozing from his nose and the side of his mouth.

17. CAB RIDE TO THE NINTH CIRCLE

I sat panting in the heat. My knee went from numb to throbbing. I left Simon where he lay and went to find his bathroom. I had to take off my trousers to examine my knee. In the dim streetlight that came in through the window, I could see it was already swollen and purplish. Lucky for me, there was only a shallow cut where the knife nicked me. I grabbed a musty washcloth and stuck it under cold running water, and held it on my knee while I sat on the closed toilet.

I had underestimated Simon. He'd taken me by surprise with the knife because of it. He was a bad aim, but probably not so bad up close and personal. I made him for The Beef's killer. But could he have done it alone? Doubtful. But Simon's little cab ride with Hamill was far from coincidence. I got up and hobbled back to the front room and found a phone.

Simon was still out cold. As I waited for the operator to pick up, I looked down at him. He breathed irregularly, his face still holding the anguish of his beating in the gloom. His cheeks and lips were swelled up like balloons. Made my knuckles hurt just looking at him.

"Hello, Operator? Can you get me the Yellow Cab Company?"

No reply but the sound of the connection over the line. Then a gruff voice.

"Yellow Cab, whatcha need?"

I raised the pitch of my voice in an attempt to disguise it.

"Hey, yeah, I need a cab right away." I gave Simon's address but changed the last number. "Ummm, listen. Is Tim Hamill working tonight? Yeah? Well, he's an old buddy. You think you could dispatch him here? My grandmother has to get to the hospital to see my old man. You can do that? Great! Thanks so much, mister." I hung up the phone. I needed Hamill back on the street, but not at Simon's address, to divert any suspicion he might have.

I stepped over Simon and walked toward his bedroom. The blackout shades were drawn. I clicked on a floor lamp and saw the room was in disarray, blankets strewn atop his bed. Girlie magazines sat open on the floor; a sticky-looking, wadded-up rag lay next to them. I opened his closet and found a bathrobe and removed the tie from the loops. "This'll work just fine," I said to myself. I turned off the light and headed back to the living room. I reached down and rolled Simon onto his face, pulled his hands behind his back and bound them together. I flipped him back over, grabbed him under his arms, and lifted him up onto the love seat. His breathing was interrupted briefly, but then resumed with a snort. I went around through the kitchen to the back door. I glanced up at Simon's wall clock. It was close to nine o'clock.

I opened the back door and walked through the dismal yard, and out to the back alley. I walked up the alley and then, just as I cut over to Nashville Avenue, I stopped. All of a sudden, this seemed like a foolish move. Sure, Hamill would be coming up the block, but then what would I do? Jump out and accost him in the middle of the street with my gun? Too many kids playing stickball still out, darkness be damned. I shook my head. All the crap I'd been involved in the last two days must have addled me. I turned around and headed back down the alley to Simon's.

The street lights were on—the ones that worked, anyway. I reentered through the back door and reached Simon's front room to wait. I didn't turn on any lights and the windows were closed, which made me crabby. My stomach started growling, too. I checked my watch: 9:25. Hamill should have been here by now. I looked back at Simon. He was still out cold. I wondered if I'd gone too far in pummeling him with my fists. Nah, I thought. I walked over and picked up the phone again to call Yellow Cab.

"Yeah, I called about a cab over a half-hour ago. Well, the driver isn't here yet. And my grandmother's getting nervous about getting over to the hospital. It being late and all. She's afraid they won't let her...."

The dispatcher broke in. "I remember you. We couldn't get ahold of Tim Hamill. We're sending another driver."

"What do you mean?" I changed my tone and resumed the higher pitch, having forgotten about disguising my voice. Guess that didn't work anyway. "Isn't he working tonight?"

"He should be, buddy, but he's not answering the radio. You want the cab or not?"

My nervous system reminded me of how much it loves to be in my body. I felt my heart flutter and my chest tighten.

"Uh, yeah. It's just ... never mind. We'll figure somethin' else out." I hung up and looked at Simon. Hamill's flat above the bakery was less than a mile from here. I made up my mind to leave Simon and hope he didn't come to while I was gone. I slipped out the back door and headed back to the alley. I figured I'd take the alley up the block to stay more hidden, then loop around to get to my car. But just then, I caught a pair of headlights shining down Nashville. The car stopped in front of Simon's. I hurried back to the worn-out garage and pressed myself against one side of it, hoping it wouldn't choose now to collapse. I risked a look along the breezeway. All I could see was the front end of the car out in the street. Its headlights were still on, and I couldn't tell the make for the darkness, nor could I see who was driving. The driver got out and shut his car door. A few minutes passed before I heard anything else. Crouching down, my knee throbbed and felt as if the swelling was getting worse, but I knew I couldn't move. And at this point, I didn't want to go back into the house. I'd had enough confrontations for the night. Hell, I'd had enough for a lifetime. That's when I heard a voice that could have been Simon's, followed by the slam of two car doors. The car roared away, tires squealing, as the mystery driver shot up the block heading east.

I had a hunch the mystery driver was Hamill, but I couldn't be sure since I hadn't seen him. If I wanted to make sure, I needed to get to my car, fast, and follow him. I'd have to chance it that Hamill revived Simon and hustled him out of there. I hightailed it back to my car as best as I could with my gimpy leg. If I was lucky, maybe Hamill would head back to his house. Kill two birds with one stone, too. That is if Simon was actually with him.

Although my knee hurt like hell, I made it to Tamm Street and West Park in record time. I parked just outside the darkened bakery and proceeded to Hamill's apartment. I rang the buzzer and waited. Nothing happened. Peering through the door leading up to Hamill's apartment, I could see Hamill's door was ajar. Light from the apartment spilled onto the stairway landing. I opened the screen door and tried the front door. It was unlocked, so I went in and closed the door behind me.

"Hamill? Tim Hamill? You here?" No answer. I yelled again as I made my way up the stairs. As I continued, I pulled my .38 out of its holster and held it at ready in front of me.

Once on the landing, I bobbed my head around the doorway for a quick peek into Hamill's apartment. Nothing. No sound. No movement. Still pointing my gun ahead of me, I pushed the door further open with my free hand. Before I entered, I leaned back and looked through the crack where the door was hinged. Didn't want to give someone the chance to shove the door and take me by surprise. As I entered the room, I fanned my gun in a semi-circle and scanned the surroundings. All clear. That's when I saw him.

"Hamill?"

He was leaned back in a swivel chair, his eyes glazed, staring at nothing. His mouth hung open, and his tongue protruded over his lower lip. Dead. Deader than dead. Still, I felt his neck. No pulse. But he was still warm.

I holstered my .38 and gave Hamill the once-over. There was a cut on his right cheek. Not much blood. So, it couldn't have been that little nick that killed him I lifted his head off the back of the chair and examined it from all angles. Nothing there. Then I looked at him straight on. Pay dirt. His neck was red and swollen. Right over the jugular vein bruising was evident. Looked like a pair of fingerprint bruises. He'd been choked to death.

But by whom? It couldn't have been Jimmy or Kira. This time of night they would be at the bar. Then I remembered what Officer Downing had said to me: "I'm gonna be talking to him, too." Maybe he'd done it. It was possible.

He'd been mighty damn upset with me by the size of the lump he'd left on my head. Would he have motive enough to ice Hamill? And where the hell was Simon if he did leave with Hamill just now? This couldn't have been Simon's work. Without a knife, there was no threat in him.

I looked around the room. There were some signs of a struggle that could be confused with poor housekeeping. I decided that Downing hadn't been here long before he went for Hamill. Maybe Hamill made the first move. But I doubted it. Unless he was scared and threatened. Where would Downing be now? I thought of Simple Simon, bound in his own living room. Maybe I imagined Simon's voice outside his house. Now my attention returned to Downing. I couldn't fathom that he'd had time to knock off Simon before getting to Hamill. This shit was getting too confusing. I decided to risk a couple more minutes in the apartment and look around.

The place was small and not as clean as Hamill protested it was during our meeting in the bakery. A light was on over the kitchen sink, which held slimy rinse water the color of sewage. An ashtray on the countertop had spilled and Hamill hadn't bothered to clean it up. I left the kitchen and passed the bathroom. The door was wide open and it was dark inside. I could make out a claw-footed tub, but no shower curtain. One more room, the bedroom. The door was partially closed. Opening it brought some light in, but not much. Rather than risk turning on more light or getting fingerprints everywhere, I took out my Zippo and struck it above my head. The room was the one neat space in the whole apartment. One bookshelf held folded clothes. There was no closet door to be seen. The carpet looked clean and empty of refuse. At the foot of the made-up bed were two pairs of polished shoes. On top of the bed was another pair of shoes. These, however, were attached to human feet. I moved the Zippo up the length of the bed and was startled to see Simple Simon looking at me through half-closed eyes. I snapped the lighter to cut the flame. I didn't move.

After a minute of listening, I heard a snore escape from Simon. I felt my way along the side of the bed close to the exterior wall and then flicked the Zippo again. This time Simon's eyes were closed, although his left eyelid looked cracked open. Blood from his beating caked one side of his face. Had he momentarily awakened? Had he seen me? I didn't know if he could have in the light. But what the hell was he doing here? If he had been abducted by Downing, why didn't Downing finish him, instead of just dumping him here? These were too many questions to ponder in a murder victim's apartment.

I stepped back away from the bed and left the apartment. I hadn't touched anything except Hamill's neck. No time to think about that. I raced down the stairs, then peered out through the front door. There were a few pedestrians on the other side of the street, reeling and cheerful, their drunken voices testifying to their obliviousness. I opened the door with my handkerchief, wiping both knobs as I exited, and closed the door quickly behind me. I started back to my car, forcing a slow, measured pace, trying not to draw attention to myself. But when I sighted my Chevy, I broke into a trot, got in, revved her up, and drove away.

Nothing was making sense. If Downing was Hamill's killer, why didn't he do Simon, too? Why cart him over to Hamill's apartment and leave him untied on his bed? Maybe Downing was hoping Simon would stay passed out until someone discovered Hamill's body, implicating Simon. That was a big stretch, and I knew it. I also knew that Simon was somehow involved in The Beef's murder.

And Downing's actions and protests suggested he was doing a little more than necessary to clear his own name. It was time to make the trip to Broad Jimmy's again.

It was also time for me to stop pretending that I could exclude the police from my little adventure. I was smart enough to know that. I stopped at a pay phone on Mc-Causland before getting on the highway. The operator connected me with District 5, north of downtown.

"I've got information on The Beef's murder."

"Who is this?" the desk sergeant asked. He half-covered the mouthpiece and told someone in the background to shut the fuck up.

"Not tellin'. Go to Broad Jimmy's tavern. Downtown."

"I know where it is. Now who is this?"

"Ixnay. Broad Jimmy's. The answer to The Beef's murder."

I hung up before he could ask me who the hell I was again. I hoped that was enough to get some law down there. I was going to need it.

I pulled onto Locust for what felt like the hundredth time in the last twenty-four hours. I parked a block away from Broad Jimmy's and kept in the shadows away from the streetlights. There wasn't much activity on the block. Just a passing bus and some guy on a motorcycle. I checked my watch: 10:15. There should be a few people entering or exiting the bar at this hour. But there wasn't a soul around. As I came up to the alley next to Broad Jimmy's, I looked up but didn't see any light from either of the windows along the fire escape. And I noticed along the front of the building, the neon lights in the windows of the tavern were turned off. A surge of adrenaline reunited with my muscles.

I knew if I peered in the front window, I could be spotted. So, I turned down the alley and walked over to the kitchen door. It was locked. I didn't want to make a clatter with the

fire escape ladder, so getting up to the upper floors was a
no go. I came back onto the sidewalk. Just as I came back
around to the front of the tavern, a car made the turn off
Locust and started down towards the tavern. I withdrew to
the shadows and waited for the car to pass, but it stopped
instead. I poked my head around the corner. The car, a late-
model Buick, idled in front of Broad Jimmy's. I could see
the silhouette of the driver, but no one else appeared to be
in the car. The engine cut off. The driver's door opened, and
the dome light confirmed he was alone. I couldn't see his
face as he got out and walked to the back of the car. He
ran his fingers along the trunk and mumbled to himself, so
he stopped and turned around, opened his door, leaned in
and grabbed at something. When he came around again,
he gripped a revolver that he held alongside his leg. As he
approached the door, the light over the entrance revealed
who it was. Officer Downing, wearing plain clothes. He
seemed to listen for a moment, then yanked on the handle
and burst inside, gun leading the way. If any time was my
chance, this was it. I counted to five to steady myself, then
ran out of the alley, my own revolver already in my hand.
I pushed open the door and stormed in, just as Officer
Downing had.

This was the scene: the bar was empty and dimly lit,
save for the colored lights above the bar mirror. Officer
Downing whirled around to face me. There didn't seem to
be anyone else around, but I wasn't able to take an inven-
tory as Downing pointed his gun at me and cocked it.

"Downing, it's Ed Darvis. Don't shoot. Don't shoot!" I
spoke in a hissing whisper that gained an octave. He kept
the gun on me, and his expression didn't change. Then
oddly, he brought a finger up to his lips and jerked his
head towards the red curtain that separated the bar from

the kitchen. I stayed glued to my spot and listened. Then I heard a female voice, muffled, so I couldn't understand what was being said. It might have been Kira, but her voice sounded high and sing-songy. After a moment, I realized it was her, and that she was speaking Japanese.

Downing seemed to notice my gun for the first time. His eyes widened behind his glasses, then narrowed. I pointed the gun at the floor and raised my left hand in a gesture of no-harm. He raised two fingers in a victory sign, then pointed with the same hand at the red curtains. I understood him to mean two people and I nodded. I crept closer to him. He kept his gun on me and watched.

I got close enough to him to whisper. He was tense and sweating. "Officer, what's going on?"

He held the gun steady, almost touching it to my gut.

"Kira Harto is back there. With her brother."

He spoke so quietly I wasn't sure I heard him right. Brother? What brother? In all the years I'd known Jimmy and Kira, I never heard anything about a brother.

"Look," I whispered, as though ignoring what he had said. "I was just by Tim Hamill's place. Yeah, the cabbie." I waited to see how he would react. His expression betrayed nothing.

"He's dead. Strangled."

He only nodded and looked at me as though I had read him yesterday's headline.

"You do it?" I asked. There's no way to be nonchalant with that question.

"No," he whispered. He was trembling slightly. Another voice in the kitchen distracted us. It was a man's voice, also speaking in Japanese. Kira interrupted him, but the man I assumed was her brother shouted over her. Then we heard a smack. The brother must have slapped his sister. Or knowing Kira, the other way around. Then silence.

I raised my eyebrows at Downing. He turned from me and tiptoed to the hinged part of the bar top. I came to his side as he raised it. When it was up, he held up three fingers. He folded his ring finger down, and I nodded in understanding. Next came his middle finger. As he folded his pointer I grasped the curtain and yanked it aside. Downing pushed through the entrance and yelled, "Police! Hands up! Don't move! Do not move!"

I jumped in alongside him and also yelled, "Don't move!" I felt a little foolish, even in the midst of the adrenaline wash. Downing was in charge.

Kira Harto, dressed to the nines under an immaculate apron, her mouth agape, stood there in shock. Her brother cowered in front of her, clutching his jaw.

"Hands up!" Officer Downing commanded. "Now!" Seeing our revolvers, both complied. I backed up into the doorway. The curtains pestered me and I yanked them down, not taking my eyes off the two.

"Hands on top of your heads. Do it! Now, come this way. Slowly. I said slow!"

Downing backed up beside me. I, too, backed up into the main room and pulled out two chairs. Downing stayed behind the bar while Kira and her brother walked toward me. Downing waved his gun toward the chairs. "Now, sit!" They did, their hands still on top of their heads. "Sit on your hands. All the way under! Under!" Kira looked up at me. I expected to see hatred, but her eyes were blank, like someone staring off into space. Her brother whimpered and said something in Japanese.

Keeping my gun pointed in Kira's direction, I told Downing I was going to lock the door. I didn't know where Jimmy or Simple Simon were, or, for that matter, where anyone else who was involved in this might be. Last thing I needed was someone like my Uncle Charles to come wobbling through the door.

I came back to Downing's side. Kira was composed. Which suggested she wasn't going to say much. She was smart enough not to implicate herself in anything. Her brother, on the other hand, I wasn't so sure. He continued to whimper, and maybe not just because of the slap. He looked like a child who had just broken the cookie jar and then stepped on a shard just as his Mommy walked in. Fat tears laid on his cheeks. He mumbled something in Japanese, drawing a harsh look from Kira, along with a rebuke. Downing focused his attention on Kira.

"Now, Miss Harto. Start from the beginning. And I better hear the truth."

Kira looked from me to Officer Downing and then shrugged. With her hands tucked under her thighs, she looked like a schoolgirl. Not an innocent one, but one who knows which boy stole from the teacher, and how she would blackmail him.

"The whole truth?" she sneered.

"You know what I mean," Downing snapped. I didn't. So I was anxious to hear what she had to say.

I cut in and pointed my gun at the whimpering man. "Just to be sure, Kira, who's he?" Downing looked at me like I was an idiot.

"He's my brother. Ichiro. Say hello to the nice detective, Ichiro." Ichiro didn't respond. He kept sulking, his head down. She yelled something in Japanese, and then he looked at me with bleary eyes. "Heh-roh," he managed. Kira smiled at me. "Trouble with his r's."

A switch went off in my head and sent a cool message down my spine. Trouble with his r's. Why was that familiar?

Had someone mentioned that to me recently? My mind fluttered and failed me.

"Enough of that." Downing broke in. "Spill it."

"All right, Officer. My brother is here from California. He's been in Missouri for six months. It didn't take him long to get a nice job. With Yellow Cab." She looked at me again and smiled—the smile of an executioner. "He got to know Tim Hamill very well. Tim trained him, and he wasn't too much of a bastard to a, a slant-eye, right? You see, we—Tim and my brother—and I—all had something in common. George Reynolds."

I didn't understand why she was so quick to tip that much. Then, I glanced over at Officer Downing. He'd turned pale.

Kira continued. "In contrast to my brother, who, as you can see, is a rather meek young man, George Reynolds was a brute. And not just in the boxing ring. Did you know that he served in World War II, Officer Downing? You must have been a little boy then. But he didn't go overseas. He was stationed in California, policing an internment camp. You know what those were, don't you? Where they kept all those pesky little Japs who might support the enemy? I doubt your comic books told you as much."

Downing's face reddened. "Make it good, Kira," he said lamely. His non sequitur only seemed to empower her further.

She continued to smile, although it was more a smirk. "Oh, it's good, Officer Downing. You see, George Reynolds, the bastard, took a shine to my mother. She was in the camp. Ichiro was just seven years old then—old enough to know things were bad. Only he didn't know how bad. Until he began to hear things at night. Our *okasan*. Crying. A man's voice—a loud, obnoxious American voice—yelling and cursing at my mother when she didn't do what he wanted. And he heard him slap her. Beat her." Kira had stopped smiling.

I didn't know how much English Ichiro understood, but he had stopped whimpering and stared at the floor, as if in a trance.

"Reynolds had her—took my mother—for close to a year. Almost every night, except those nights when another woman was his prey. And on those nights, Ichiro and our *okasan* held each other. And waited, in the dark. Afraid. Always afraid. Would he come tonight anyway? Would she be given a night of reprieve? But they were not alone. There was a girl there, Ichiro's sister. She was older than him by eight years. She, too, heard the slaps, the cries of pain. Fear. She was old enough to know what was happening and she shielded her brother from that knowledge. That their mother was abused, raped. But it was hard to keep up."

Downing and I kept our guns rigid in front of us. I felt like a hostile audience slowly thrust into doubt at some avant-garde play. And I was in awe that Kira spoke of herself as if she weren't there. That the girl in the camp was someone else.

Kira continued. "Eventually, George Reynolds was replaced by another soldier. This one had returned from a tour of duty in the Pacific. He was so bent on destroying the Japanese, no matter they were Americans, that he did a turn at the internment camp. But he was different. He didn't have eyes for our mother. The daughter, she was fifteen and beautiful. She learned and spoke English very well when studying in Hong Kong, at a British-run academy, where she lived until she was eight."

"Why Hong Kong?" I croaked. My throat was dry. I realized I hadn't swallowed since Kira began her tale.

"Mr. Darvis, my father was an esteemed researcher,

and his work took him internationally. Just because I'm Japanese doesn't mean I'm strictly from Japan. But do you really care?" She examined me, her mouth a flat line. I could stamp Ugly American on my forehead later.

"I apologize," I said, finding my voice. "Please, continue."

"This other man, he came at night and took the daughter instead. But he was gentle. No slaps. No harsh words. And because the mother was spared the violence, and the brother was no longer scared, the daughter let the soldier think that he had seduced her. That she might love him. When the war ended and we Japanese-Americans were set free, with no money, no jobs, no homes, he offered to provide a home for the daughter's family in California. But under one condition. That the daughter be his bride and return with him to a city she had never heard of before—St. Louis.

"The offer was too good to refuse. The offer could not be refused. And at their separation, the daughter promised her mother's son that she would send for him. When he was older. When he was a man." She paused a moment. "And revenge could be served."

Kira had resumed all the loveliness and poise of this morning. When I asked, "So, how does Tim Hamill fit into this?" it sounded inane.

"Like I told you, he trained Ichiro to drive a cab. And he also knew George Reynolds. The Beef fought Hamill's father in the late forties. He'd knocked him out while they fought in the ring. Gave him a concussion. The concussion led to a coma days later. Hamill's father became a vegetable. What more do you need to know, Detective?"

I looked at her and then at Officer Downing. His gun had moved from Kira and her brother to me.

"What's this? We're on the same side here."

"Drop your gun." His face was again pale, and he was

sweating profusely. I crouched down slowly with the gun extended out from my body. "Drop it!" he yelled. I let go of it inches from the floor and stood back up. "Now, sit down. Sit! Sit!" He was borderline hysterical. I pulled out a chair and sat down next to Ichiro, who continued to stare at the floor. It was as if he hadn't registered anything that had been said.

Kira spoke again. "Won't you let me finish my story, Officer Downing?"

I studied her face. The composure. The secret knowledge. Despite the danger of Downing's gun, I felt moved by her story and her beauty, as though the two together might save this recondite and damned world.

"You've said enough," Downing muttered.

"I haven't heard nearly enough," I volunteered.

"You shut up!" Downing ordered.

"Why not let him hear it? Since you're the only one pointing the gun here now, what will it hurt if I continue?"

Downing looked as though he didn't know what to do. He looked outside the window, then returned his attention to each of us. I thought about the call I had made to the police station. Now would be a good time for the cops to show up. Kira took Downing's silence as the advantage to keep talking.

"You see, Detective, many people had reason to want George Reynolds dead. Even Officer Downing here."

"You shut up!" Downing shouted. He brought back a hand to strike Kira. She looked up at Downing and held still. She didn't even flinch.

Downing slowly lowered his hand, and when he did she yelled, "No, I won't! You're just as guilty as my brother! As guilty as Simple Simon! As guilty—" She never got to finish. Downing struck Kira with the butt of his gun. She recoiled from the blow and closed her eyes. Ichiro's spell was broken. He began weeping again.

Now, Downing's chest heaved, and he issued a ragged breath. My gun lay on the floor a foot away from me. If only I were just a little closer. Downing must have sensed my thoughts. He pointed his gun at me and came forward, and then kicked my .38 to the other side of the room. He stepped back to the open space where the hinged bar top still stood open. That's when I heard a noise from the kitchen. Downing didn't seem to notice.

"Now what?" I asked plainly, trying to distract him.

"Just be quiet!" Downing barked.

"Officer, if you're involved with The Beef's murder, just tell me about it. I'm in the truth business, remember?"

"I got nothin' to say."

"I don't believe you killed him."

"What?" The front of his dress shirt was dark with sweat.

"I said, I don't believe you killed him. Whatever happened in that alley, I don't think you were the one who killed The Beef."

He stared at me as though dazed. I continued.

"I don't think you were around for any noble purpose, either. But you weren't the knife man. Whatever the reason, it's not important to me. The Beef was the kind of guy who would give anyone who knew him murderous thoughts. If he crossed you, or did you wrong, I don't believe anyone on the force would think twice about you giving him a little sap in a dark alley."

Downing's lip trembled. "I—" He couldn't form words for a moment. "I just wanted to teach him a lesson. That blowhard son-of-a-bitch! Talkin' about my wife that way! He doesn't even know her! Then I thought, what if he did? Did he come near her? Threaten her?" His face looked waxen, hastily molded atop a skull.

I nodded sympathetically. If I could just keep him talking. A shadow moved in the kitchen. With his back turned, Downing didn't notice.

"I came home that night and couldn't sleep. My wife was asleep in the bed and all I could do was stare at her and wonder. I got so mad, I got in my car and came back down here. I didn't want to kill him. I just wanted to hurt him. Let him know it was not okay for him to talk about my wife. I didn't care if he knew who it was. I wanted to hurt him."

"Then what happened?"

"I walked down the block and came up to the alley. That's when I saw the body. I didn't know it was The Beef. Until he tried to sit up. That scared the hell out of me. I saw it was him. I just stood there. He got to his knees. And when he raised up, he held his hand to his neck. His throat was cut. He was gurgling. Reaching out to me. I came towards him, and … and … something snapped. I…."

"You what?" I asked without malice.

"I walked around behind him and I hit him over the head. Twice. He fell over on his face. Then I panicked. I bolted out from the alley, and there was the cab. Hamill saw me. I ran. I just ran. I couldn't stop. God!" He brought his free hand up and rubbed his jaw, and then wiped his eyes. Kira's eyelids fluttered open. She raised her head and looked dazedly at Downing.

"He was already done for. You did him a favor," I said.

"No, he wasn't. Maybe he would have lived."

"Not with his throat sliced ear to ear. Another minute and he would have bled to death anyway."

"But he was alive when I got to him."

"Hardly. Actually, you helped him along. You put him out

of everybody's misery."

"I can't think that."

"Officer Downing. The police will be here any time. I don't think anyone here is going to say a word about your involvement. Let us go, and our lips are sealed."

"No," Kira said. Downing looked at her, hatred replacing the confusion on his face.

"What did you say?" he demanded.

"I said no. You're going to take the fall for The Beef's death."

"Like hell I am, you Jap bitch! Your brother's the one who did it! And he's gonna hang for it!"

"What proof do you have?" Kira asked coolly. "You just confessed your involvement in the murder. My brother had nothing to do with it. You're going to let us go, and we're going back to the happy life we've made."

"Not if I can help it!" Downing turned the gun on Kira. In the same instant that I was going to yell out to stop him, Broad Jimmy emerged in the doorway to the kitchen. He looked like some zombie creature, crazed with bloodlust in the dimness. He reached both his arms around Downing's torso and lifted him off the ground. Downing's gun fired once before it fell out of his slack hand. I could see Jimmy's face change as he began to squeeze. Downing gasped once, going pale.

"Jimmy," I said as calmly as I could. He ignored me and kept the pressure on Downing's rib cage. I heard a crackling sound, followed by another. A stricken moan escaped Downing's lips. A bit of froth came sputtering out.

"Jimmy," I said again, louder. "Jimmy, don't. Don't kill him. Jimmy! He's a cop, for chrissakes!" I stood up. Kira lunged for me and knocked me down. She kicked at me with high heels. I grabbed one of them before it made contact with my face and shoved upward. She went down on her ass and her head hit the table behind her. She lay still. I heard a sickening crunch in the quiet after her fall. I looked Jimmy's way and grimaced. He had snapped Downing's neck. It was as if he couldn't see Kira on the floor or her idiot brother sobbing in his chair, his hands still under him, or me sitting in front of his chair. He held onto Downing's body for a moment. Then he let him fall. That's when Jimmy seemed to register that Kira was on the floor. He stepped over Downing. A look of tenderness came over Jimmy's face. He stood over her.

"Kira," he croaked. He got down on his knees and lifted her up. She was like a toddler in his arms. I stood and backed away from them. Somehow I remembered the locked door. I walked over and unlocked it. As I came back to them, the first sirens wailed in the distance. I steered clear of Jimmy and Kira. He was beginning to sob now, too, great big bear sobs. A loud crier. He drowned out Ichiro, the worthless, blubbering lump who was just a boy, not a man. Not even a murderer, perhaps.

I saw red and blue lights play across the dim walls of the tavern. I retrieved my gun and shoved it into my jacket pocket right before the door flew open and three police officers filed in, guns drawn. When they saw us, they trained their weapons on all of us. They looked like a commercial for the police academy. After all I'd witnessed the past two days, though, I just didn't have the stomach for sarcasm. I raised my hands and waited for the rigamarole to begin.

18. THE EYES OF KIRA HARTO

Twenty minutes later, Broad Jimmy was cuffed and sitting in the back of a squad car. Kira's brother had already been brought in for questioning. Kira herself would need a trip to the hospital, followed by her own round of questioning. I hoped she kept to the same story, and that it was the truth. It felt like the truth. All I didn't know was if her brother had the grit to be The Beef's cutter. Sure didn't seem likely.

Officer Downing's body was covered, lifted onto a stretcher, and taken away into the night. He, too, got a free ride to the hospital—to its air-conditioned bottom floor, that is.

I was the only one who didn't need a doctor. At least, not the care of a doc at City Hospital. I remained at the tavern and told a cop new to me, Detective Fleischman, everything I knew. Except for two things. I didn't mention that I was one of The Beef's body haulers. I only said that I didn't know where the body was, and that was the truth. I also didn't say anything about Officer Downing's role in The Beef's death. I had seen the slice in his neck. Downing probably thought he was the linchpin, but I didn't. And I kept my story that way. It was a risk, considering that Kira was hot to pin the whole thing on Downing. But it would be her word against mine. And her idiot brother had been near catatonic throughout the whole ordeal. Call it a favor to Downing. From one man who understands another's rage very well.

I was released an hour after the police arrived. I made a couple of meaningful promises to be in touch and not to think about leaving town any time soon. Fine. I'd cancel my ticket for the French Riviera then.

I walked up to Locust, away from the gawkers, the press photographers, and police cars. I found my car. Some nice guy had parked so close to my front bumper that I had to rock the car in reverse and first several times to get out of the space. I resisted the temptation to key the side of his car. I'd had enough of vengeance for one day.

I crossed Grand to Kingshighway and then headed toward my apartment building in the West End. The music store downstairs was darkened. In my hallway, I heard quiet music coming from the artist's apartment, along with some other noise inside. I unlocked my door and switched on the overhead light. I didn't expect any surprises, and for once, reality met my expectations. I closed and locked the door. I didn't even have the energy to make a night cap. I urinated, washed my face, and stripped to my T-shirt and boxers. I had left a fan on in my bedroom, which made it somewhere shy of bearable. Bearable enough to sleep like the dead.

I woke up the next morning with the snap of Officer's Downing's neck in my ears. I felt grouchy, despite having slept until ten. Things felt unfinished. The Beef was dead. The cabbie Tim Hamill was dead. Officer Downing was dead. Broad Jimmy was done for, and would probably face life without parole. That left Kira's brother, Ichiro. Was he The Beef's killer? Then, of course, there was Kira herself.

Could she have pulled this off? Years of desire for vengeance and her smarts made it plausible. Jimmy loved her for real. She just may have put on an act with him all these years to get back at George Reynolds, but fifteen years is a long time for someone to star in shadow theater. And finally, Simple Simon. He was in contact with Hamill. Kira had said something to him in the tavern that caused him to bolt out of there, refusing to talk to me. But I had laid him out during the time Tim Hamill was choked of his last breath—at least I thought. Simon had better be conscious today and ready to talk. Momentarily, and in a sick way, I was glad the first human being he'd see upon waking would be Tim Hamill, rigid in his easy chair.

I put coffee on to brew and made some toast. I didn't have the appetite for much more. I contemplated going into the office, or contacting the Five to get any word from Detective Fleischman. But I decided the hell with that. Instead, I went downstairs and out the front door onto the sidewalk. It was cloudy. Still humid, but a breeze from the west blew along the boulevard. Let it rain, I thought. Hard. I got a morning paper and pack of cigarettes from the corner shop. Back inside my apartment, I searched the paper for any mention of the "missing" George Reynolds or Officer Downing's death. There was nothing. Too late in the night for the downtown scribes to put it in. There was a sidebar on Tim Hamill's death, however. Seems he'd been strangled in his apartment by an unknown intruder. Nothing stolen. A man found sleeping in Hamill's bed was taken into custody. Currently, police had no motive and were investigating. The usual inkwell drained of blackened bullshit when there were no leads.

I read through the whole paper and pretended to care how the Cardinals were doing. I read the op-ed pages, columnists alternately smearing and elevating John F. Kennedy, and moaning about Cuba. The usual letters to the editor about traffic problems, Civil Rights. I even looked at the damned real estate section and dreamed about a little cabin down on the Current River, or a piece of property deep in the Ozarks. I grew bored, restless, and then sleepy.

At around four in the afternoon the phone rang. I woke slowly, not wanting to rouse up out of my stupor. My mouth tasted like burnt coffee laced with ashes. I had been leaning in the chair on my right arm, and it still smarted from Officer Downing's night-stick attack. I picked up the phone with my left hand.

"Mr. Darvis? This is Detective Fleischman."

Courtesy from a cop. Put that in the papers tomorrow.

"I'm here. What have you got for me?"

"You sitting down? This may take awhile."

"Sure, I'm sitting. You told me to stay close. I haven't really budged from my apartment."

He gave a gruff chuckle. Simon was up, but not necessarily at 'em. When he found out where he was and what had happened, he caved, Fleischman said. The grey-bearded songbird. Kira had meant to rely on her brother and Tim Hamill to finish The Beef. On a predictable night, when The Beef would be the last person at the bar, maybe assisted with some free drinks from Kira, she would call Hamill directly. He would pick up Ichiro, and they would come down to the tavern. It was important to the timing that Kira allow The Beef to leave, hoping that he would be too wasted to go far, it seems. Seems, too, they'd made two previous, unsuccessful attempts. The first time, The Beef had strayed too far for them to find him. The second time, when they had the perfect opportunity, Ichiro got cold feet and couldn't go through with it. That figures, I thought.

That's when Kira decided not to rely on her mousy brother for the job anymore. And when she approached Simon, she let on that she had a thing for him. She may have made sexual promises, as well. Whatever charms she offered, Simon became the willing cut-man. On the third attempt, the night The Beef was successfully murdered, just Simon and Hamill were at the scene. After Simon sliced The Beef in the alley, he got into Ichiro's cab, which was parked on a side street, and the two got away. Hamill must have pulled around the block and then "found" the body, I figured. Detective Fleischman didn't mention anything about Officer Downing showing up unplanned after Simon sliced The Beef's throat and adding his contribution to his death. I didn't know if he was leaving that part out, or that he just didn't know. And I wasn't about to ask. I was already in some trouble with the law for knowing about the crime and not going to the police. I waited to hear if Fleischman knew I helped Broad Jimmy with the meat-packing job, but he never mentioned that, either.

"So far, so good," I muttered.

"What's that?" Fleischman asked.

"Hm? Oh, nothing. So far it makes sense," I responded.

Fleischman continued. The next morning, Hamill and Simon came back for The Beef's body. It was then that Kira had drugged Broad Jimmy. Which now makes sense why the bar was closed. Simon, cooperating with Hamill, weighted The Beef's body and dropped it in the Missis-sippi, somewhere upriver and out of sight. They might have to send divers for a look-see, Fleischman said. They'd more likely find a guy in cement slippers before finding The Beef, but who knows? Simple Simon hadn't said anything about my involvement. Yet. Unwittingly, I had helped Kira with The Beef's disposal. If she talked, I was looking at jail time as an accomplice. But then again, she was looking at worse.

On top of everything else, I wasn't getting paid for this little venture. There's always that risk, especially with a squirrelly client—or with a client likely heading to Gumbo. A payout just wasn't in the cards for me this time. Even if I had been paid, a hundred bucks would come nowhere close in matching the risk to my life and limb. Maybe I'm just too efficient. Or, maybe I'm just not that smart.

"We're going to need you to come downtown and answer some more questions, Darvis. Corroborate a few things," Fleischman said. Nothing in his tone suggested I was in deeper trouble. But the earlier courtesy from him was gone.

"I'll be there in an hour. And thanks," I said before hanging up. I sat in the armchair and stretched out my right arm, trying to relieve the muscle pain. The shackles on my wrists had left their mark, too, and I shook myself to clear the feeling. A shower and some food could only delay the inevitable station visit. And I had one call to make before I left. I dialed St. Mary's Hospital.

If it was possible to feel any lower, more dependent, or helpless, I haven't known it. For all I've tried to do these last few days, I've seen too many people killed. I haven't been able to stop two clients from committing the crime of murder. I've broken the law, acted cavalier, hurt my body, and pissed off a few cops. I've uncovered more human stupidity, selfishness, and greed, and still wasn't able to do anything about it. And my role in these dark and dumb proceedings might lead me to lose my license, and even do some time.

"Bertie? It's Ed. Yeah. Well, not so good. You? You sure? This a bad time? You weren't sleeping or anything? Listen,

I'm gonna need a good lawyer. Yeah, I mean it. Well, let me tell you all about it."

My visit with Fleischman was surprisingly short. When I arrived at the station he informed me that Bertie Albanese had phoned him on my behalf. He made a few mild jibes about me, and my relationship with Bertie. But whatever Bertie had said did the trick. Fleischman treated me like a peer. A couple of times, as I laid out for him how Broad Jimmy had hired me, I felt a rush to confess that I had helped move the body. But I didn't. I'd already filled Bertie in, so I saw no reason to say it all again. That's the thing about the sacrament of confession: you can wash away your sins and be absolved of any wrong doing. But sometimes it means splashing those sins right into somebody else's face. And I really wasn't up to that. So, I decided to keep it between me and Bertie. And I wanted to see what Fleischman knew. Any mention of my role with the body disposal never came up.

Fleischman released me but again reminded me not to leave town. I would be subpoenaed to appear at Broad Jimmy's trial. As I stood up to go, Fleischman gripped my arm, not hard, but tight enough to be meaningful nonetheless. I looked at him as he brought his face close to mind. The friendly dark sparkle in his eyes had cooled.

"You're lucky you have a friend in Bertie Albanese. Don't forget that."

"Don't I know it," I said, and nodded at Fleischman. Some unspoken acknowledgment passed between us. Fleischman was warning me. He knew I was involved in The Beef's disappearance. Or he suspected I wasn't telling him everything, and I thought again of the lion giving one last warning to the lion tamer through the pressure of its jaws: I'm not taking your head off this time. But next time.... I didn't offer Fleischman my hand as I left. Such gestures of civility are empty at a moment like that.

As I drove back home, a few spare raindrops hammered my windshield before turning into a torrent, vengeful ghouls against the glass, every one a person I've let down or let die. I pictured Hamill sitting in his chair, dead, his throat bulging and bruised, until his half-lidded eyes suddenly spring wide, leaking blood, and he lunges for me to unite with him in death. I struck my fists against the wheel and then one against my head to shake the macabre image. I still didn't know who killed him. I was inclined to believe Officer Downing didn't do it. His motive for wanting to kill The Beef was pretty weak to begin with. He had the opportunity in the alley. He had the means with his nightstick. But motive? Talking trash about someone's wife is never an invitation to a night of dancing and fine wine, but I didn't think Downing was going back to Broad Jimmy's to kill The Beef. To teach him a lesson, yes, but more than anything he ran afoul of Kira's plan right at the time it was actually being executed. The secret to comedy might be in the timing, but in my business, it's no secret that timing more often leads to tragedy.

A tremendous crash of thunder and a fresh doubling of the downpour distracted me from any more philosophizing. I cursed my flimsy wipers and their deteriorating rubber. Looks like I'd have to delay replacing them after this case. I had to get off the highway at Jefferson and take surface streets back home. Some of them were washed out. Stalled cars blocked one or two low-lying spots. By the time I got home, nearly an hour after I had left the downtown station, my nerves were shot and my right arm was killing me. I was in a killing mood myself. Soon enough I'd have a bottle of gin in my sights.

I parked in the garage, grateful I didn't have to play the parking game out on the flooded streets. I climbed the back stairs to my hallway, glad to be out of the rain. The overhead light at the top of the stairs had been replaced, but now, the one at my end of the hall was out. Figures, I thought. Didn't really matter, though. I'd always said I could find my way blindfolded to my apartment. Hell, I've certainly done it blind drunk before. Tonight, though, I was glad for the bit of grey light pouring in through the lone window that overlooked the street. Just as I got to my door, a flash of lightning spotlighted the dingy, white walls and the thinning green carpet. As I found the lock and drove the key in, another flash of lightning brought my attention to the carpet in front of my door. A fresh set of wet footprints greeted me. I backed up and felt for the wall behind me. Another lightning flash revealed that there were two sets of footprints leading from the stairway to my door. Knowing I only had two feet, I realized that someone had come to visit and might not have left.

I automatically reached for my .38, which, of course, I had left at home when I went for my little interrogation with Detective Fleischman. In one quick motion, I faced the door, turned the key in the lock, and kicked the door open. I immediately swirled around away from the door, and plastered myself against the hallway wall and waited, more tense than ever. I could hear the box fans whirring in my apartment, no doubt sucking in rainwater, but nothing else. I ducked my head around into the doorway real quick, then retreated again in a flash, processing the glimpse of my living room and part of the kitchen. Nothing. The door swung back a little with its own momentum. It was too dark to see through the crack of the door hinge, so I crouched down and duck-walked forward, easing the door open as I did. If anyone was behind the door he was awfully patient. I sprang up, ready to attack as I swung the door toward me. No one was there. I immediately turned around and scanned the apartment. No sign of anyone. With my right fist reared back, I slammed the door with my other hand and tensed even more. No one there. I tiptoed over to the end table next to my armchair and pulled out my .38, checked the chamber mechanically, and then walked through the house, flipping on the lights in every room. I was just about to open the kitchen cabinet doors, and maybe even knock over the oven, when there was a knock on my front door.

I tensed again, and searing pain shot down my arm. I shook it off. I don't get many visitors, but I've also never had a polite intruder. Even so, and with thoughts of Downing's surprise visit yesterday still fresh, I approached the door with my gun leveled at its center.

"Who is it?" I asked. I croaked like a sick frog.

"Ed? That you?"

At first I couldn't place the voice. "Yeah, it's me. Who is it?" I kept the gun pointed forward.

"It's your neighbor, Holland."

My artist-neighbor. I let out a loud breath and felt my body relax, pouring its tension into my gun hand. I hadn't realized it until I lowered my right arm that it was beginning to shake. A spasm shot down the length of my arm to my fingertips. I pocketed my gun, wiped my face with my handkerchief, and blew out another hard breath of air.

"Hold on a minute." I shook out my arms and opened the door.

Holland stood there looking damp and unhappy. His

longish hair was wet and slicked back, a few drops falling off his nonetheless handsome face onto his dark suit, open collar, some kind of silver medallion around his neck.

"What's up?" I asked. I had to look up a little to meet his eyes. He was a pretty big guy.

"Hell, man, I got locked out. I have an opening tonight and I was loading some pieces in my friend's car."

"Why're you all wet?"

"We were leaving the block when I remembered a sculpture I'd left behind. I told him just to wait, and I made a dash for it in the rain. Didn't think I'd get this wet." He grinned at his appearance. I wasn't ready to grin at mine.

"The Super around?" I asked.

"I just checked. His office is locked up. Shit. Of all nights."

"I'm sorry about that, Holland. What can I do?"

Holland looked at his watch. "Damn. At this point, nothing. If I don't leave now, I'll be late. So, I'm gonna just have to forget about that piece. It's a shame, too. An erotic little number."

I smiled at that. "Yeah, I'm sorry, too. Can I offer you a towel or something? How 'bout a drink?"

"I'll take the towel. My buddy's waitin' in the car."

"All right. Hang on a minute."

As I walked away, Holland said, "Hey, maybe I'll take that drink later on. You gonna be up around ten?"

"That's up to the gin," I said.

Holland laughed. "All right. Tell you what, you let me borrow a towel, and I'll be back later tonight with a fresh bottle—and your towel."

"You got a deal," I said before going into the bathroom. At once, the idea of a normal neighborly visit gave me a surge of joy and relief. I could have the ordinary night I didn't even deserve. Maybe the ghosts would haunt somebody else.

I gave him the towel and he thanked me. I closed the door and locked it, still feeling overly cautious, but a helluva lot more relaxed than a few minutes before. I stashed the .38 back in the side table drawer and went to the bathroom to take a leak and wash my face. As I walked back into the bedroom to turn off the box fan, I kicked off my shoes. The window sill in front of the fan was wet, but that looked like the extent of it. No water on the floor or, worse, the bed.

Next, I headed straight to the kitchen. On the double for a double. I grabbed a cigarette, even whistled a little tune as I poured myself a glass of gin. By the time I got a cigarette lit and had a slug of gin in me, I crashed into my easy chair. I wasn't ready to call life good, but this moment would do.

I pulled on the cigarette, enjoying my respite, and certainly enjoying the waning of the storm. With the lightning, now more distant and intermittent, and the thunder just a sated growl far in the distance, I relaxed and mused. Hamill, Hamill, Hamill. Who killed you? My brain matched my body's fatigue. I needed to eat. I decided to fry up a hamburger and boil some potatoes. I'd ease up on the gin, too. Brew coffee instead. What the hell, I'd stay awake for Holland later.

It was around eight o'clock after I'd eaten. I didn't have the concentration for reading, so I clicked on the TV and let a situation comedy dull my wits further. At nine, I turned off the TV and put on a jazz record to keep me conscious. I splashed a little bourbon in my coffee to liven things up a little, too. I sat. I paced. I scribbled on a crossword puzzle from the morning paper.

At ten, there were three rapid knocks on the door. Damn, for an artist Holland possesses no sense of fashionable lateness. I unlocked the door, and as I did I could swear I caught a whiff of perfume. Too late to process, unfortunately.

The second I unlatched the lock, the door was forced open, and there stood Kira Harto with her brother, Ichiro. A beauty like that, wet with rain. Be still my beating heart. My confusion at her presence gave Ichiro the witty idea to force the door further open. I was off balance and stumbled back a step. Ichiro, a wary look in his eyes, stayed in the doorway while Kira stepped inside. She had a gun in her gloved hand. How neat.

19. BACK BENEATH THE BLACK BOUGHS

"Mr. Darvis, it really is a pleasure to see you. For perhaps the first time in my life," Kira said. Her gaze was even with mine, deadly. Her gun hand was steady, and she pointed the automatic right up at my chest.

"It's always been a pleasure for me, Kira. Up until now."

"Sit down, Mr. Darvis." She indicated my easy chair. I moved towards it, sitting slowly. I flicked my eyes from her to Ichiro. Any trace of meekness had left his eyes. He remained rooted in the doorway.

"Well, if you've come here to make good on my contract, the gun isn't necessary. I'll take a check."

"You're funny, detective. I guess you realize I'm not here to pay you." She turned her head slightly to Ichiro and hissed something in Japanese. Ichiro stepped forward, leaving the door open. He reached into his pocket and pulled out a length of rope.

"So, you're here to tie me up? In my own apartment? Go ahead. There's a couple bottles in the kitchen. I guess you'll need whatever liquor you can get for the tavern, now that Jimmy's put away."

"It's not liquor I'm after, and you know it." She spoke to Ichiro again. He drew out the rope and wrapped each end around his hands into a short tight rope, then snapped it taut for good measure. My heartbeat doubled and pumped ice water through my body.

"So, I'm the loose end, hunh, Kira?"

"That's right. I can't have your testimony contradict mine, Mr. Darvis." She gave some kind of command in Japanese to Ichiro. He began advancing towards me.

"Hold on a minute, Kira." I held my hand out toward both of them. "Stop right there, brother." She held her right arm up and Ichiro stopped coming toward me. He kept the rope taut between his hands. "You can at least explain a couple of things to me."

"Why bother? In a few minutes, you'll be dead. And you won't care." She let loose one wicked laugh through barely-opened lips. I grew colder.

"Yeah? And how? You're going to risk shooting me? How're you going to get away?"

"I'm not going to shoot you, Mr. Darvis. Unless I have to. Then I will. Ichiro," she began and continued in Japanese.

"Hold on! At least give me the dignity of hearing the last words of my life in English."

She grinned like the assassin she was. "Okay. Ichiro. Strangle Mr. Darvis."

Ichiro came forward again. He was three feet away from me when I looked directly in his eyes.

"You don't have it in you," I snorted. "You're a punk. A mama's boy. Just like you didn't have the balls to kill The Beef. Go back to California. You're a baby, not a killer." That last statement was a desperate final attempt. My words caused an imperceptible wrinkle in his expression. Maybe it was doubt. Maybe it was more rage.

"Oh, he has it in him. He's finally proven his worth," Kira said calmly.

And then it hit me. I pictured Hamill's bruised throat.

Ichiro. So, he wasn't a knife guy. He was a strangler. And here I was seated in my own apartment, just like Hamill.

"This isn't going to help you get away, Kira."

"Oh, I think it will."

"How the hell did you get out?"

"Jimmy posted our bail."

"And where's he?"

She grinned again. "Still in jail. He could only spring the two of us apparently."

"Kira. It doesn't have to be like this. I know that Simon killed The Beef. You're hot to pin it on Downing. Downing's dead. The only other accomplice left alive is Simon. Why not let him hang and leave me out of it."

She eyed me cooly. "Because you like justice too much."

"And you don't?"

"No. I like revenge." She turned her attention to Ichiro again. "Kill him, Ichiro. Do it!"

"I'm gonna fight him," I exclaimed.

"I'll shoot you," Kira countered.

"I'll take a bullet over a rope from this punk."

"Last words are over, Mr. Darvis. Kill him, Ichiro!"

Would I really prefer a bullet? My split-second of indecision gave Ichiro the chance to rush me and wrap the rope quickly around my neck. I got one hand in the way just as I brought my feet up. Two of my fingers hooked in the rope as I felt its pressure against my Adam's apple. Seated, I couldn't get enough force to maneuver Ichiro away. I kicked fiercely at his groin. He yelped, but kept tightening the rope, his wet hair dripping on my shirtfront. My own fingers caught in the rope were worthless. I would end up being party to my own strangulation. My vision was getting blurry. Kira had not moved from her position near the doorway, but she kept the gun on me. If I could kick Ichiro towards her I might have a chance. I tried two or three times. If only I hadn't taken my loafers off. He took the kicks. Goddamn he was strong. I was starting to see crimson and white stars in the blur of figures. This was not how I anticipated dying. I gave one last kick with my remaining strength. Just before blacking out, I saw another figure appear in the doorway. I heard a woman's scream, then my consciousness was cancelled.

I came to with someone slapping me in the face. I reached a weak hand up to grab my assailant.

"Ed? Ed!" I heard my name through the fog between conscious reality and unconsciousness. "Ed!"

I squinted and focused on the face in front of me. The slaps stopped at the same time. Holland, my neighbor. "You all right?" he called, needlessly loud, I thought dumbly.

"Yeah. I'm not 'onna do any jumpin' jacks for you." Holland's face was pure white. He appeared to be shaking, too. When I looked down I realized why. He was kneeling on Ichiro's prostrate form. Ichiro was wiggling underneath him, but he was no match for my tall neighbor. The term artistic temperament came into my fuzzy mind. I wanted to laugh, but my face felt like it was detached and hovering away from me.

"Gun," I managed.

"What?"

"Gun. I havva gun. Drawer there." I turned my eyes slowly to the left. Holland opened it and produced the .38. The way he held it between two fingers belied the shocked look on his face. "Here. Give it t' me."

Holland complied. I reached out my numb right hand and grasped the .38. I cocked it and gave what I hope was a reassuring look to Holland, then pointed the gun at Ichiro.

"Hollan', go 'head and get offa him." My throat strained on the words. My face felt a little less disembodied now, and began to throb, right along with my head. Holland got up slowly, grabbing Ichiro's rope as he stood. Ichiro, back to his old ways again, began to sob. I looked past him and saw Kira sprawled on her left side. Her eyes were closed and her gun hand was pressed underneath her. Just above her head, blood oozed out onto the carpet.

"Tie him up. Hands behind his back." My words were coming more easily, but now the constriction of my throat joined the head pain. My face was back now, too, no longer seeming to float in front of me. But it felt as if it were sealed on with a hot glue gun as the pain intensified. Most likely from the blood flow again going to my head. Holland bound Ichiro's hands. Ichiro was blubbering now, his face pressed into the carpet. He made no attempt to resist, nor did he even move.

"What'd you do to her?" I indicated Kira.

Holland looked at me like I had just caught him in something bad. I guess I had. He looked over at her, as if for the first time.

"I hit her from behind. I ... I came down the hall and saw her back to the door and, and, you were in the chair, and he was choking you. I just hit her. Right on the head. Oh my God, do you think I killed her? Oh, no!" He stepped over Ichiro and felt Kira's neck. For a moment his moist eyes were riveted to mine. At last he spoke.

"I think there's a pulse. I'm ... I'm not sure. Wait. Yes. Yes, she's breathing. Ed, what the hell is going on?"

"It's a long story, Holland." I couldn't think of standing up. "Call the operator. Ask for District 5. Ask for Detective Flashlight."

"Detective Flashlight?"

I snickered, which came out more like a snort, really. "Did I say that? Sorry. Fleischman. Fleisch-muhhhn." The word was becoming fun to say. Some painkiller chemicals were kicking into the bloodstream now.

Holland did as I asked. While he waited, I saw that there was a gin bottle and a sculpted piece of marble on the floor near Kira's feet.

"What's that?" I asked.

"Hunh?" Holland asked, a little too forcefully.

"On the ground. What is that?"

"Oh. My sculpture. The piece I forgot before. I was bringing it down to show you. I used it to—" He couldn't finish.

"Let me see it. I can't get up just now."

Holland gave me a peculiar look. Still holding the phone, he stepped past the weeping Ichiro and retrieved his sculpture. He handed it to me with utmost care, as though it were fragile and could perform no violence. But it had the weight of a shotgun. A little smeared blood stood out on top of it.

"Is this…?"

"Yeah, it is," Holland said. He raised his eyebrows and smiled, and then he looked at the floor. "Yes, thank you," he said into the phone. "May I speak to Detective Fleischman please? This is urgent."

"Nifty," I said over Holland's request. I peered closely at the detailed curvature of the sculpture: a man penetrating a woman from behind.

I told Holland to hide his sculpture and say he had used the unopened gin bottle to clock Kira instead. No sense in him going in on an obscenity charge as well. While he did that, I walked back in the bedroom, put my shoes back on, and turned on the fan in my bedroom window. If I was able to come back tonight, I'd want my room plenty cool.

Detective Fleischman arrived twenty minutes after the phone call with a uniformed cop and a plainclothes detective. They were from District 9, my territory. I recognized the plainclothes from a previous case. He didn't exactly look delighted to see me. The uniform untied Ichiro, put him in cuffs, and sat him on the loveseat while sirens drew near the building. The ambulance attendants came in next. They loaded Kira on a stretcher. She was still unconscious but stable, as far as I could tell. Stable in that her brain kept her lungs functioning. The plainclothes, whose name just washed over me, instructed the cop I didn't know to go along for the ride to Barnes Hospital. The Super arrived on the heels of the ambulance guys. His shocked and pained look told me I might need to find another place to live.

Fleischman scrutinized my face. "Do you want to see a doctor?"

"No, sir. But I wouldn't mind if you'd crack open that gin."

He nixed that idea immediately. "Evidence," he grunted.

"Wait, but I've got more in the kitchen."

He was curt. "Let's not fuck around," he said. "If you're steady enough to walk, we'll escort you to the station to process this whole mess. He can ride with us as well." He indicated Holland. Ichiro was taken away by the uniform.

The Super was the only one left. He had only been able to identify himself, and after the cops established he wasn't a witness, he was kept out of the way. As we walked out of my apartment, I asked him if he wouldn't mind locking up. He gave me a sour look.

On the way to the station Fleischman confirmed that

Broad Jimmy had posted Kira and her brother's bail through a third party. Despite his heartbreak, he came through for her. Jesus. He'll probably have to put a second mortgage on the bar—if he can. And for what, really? He still loved Kira, but couldn't he know she never loved him? Well, I'm no one to say. Maybe she grew to love him. I flashed to his messy separate bedroom and thought differently.

Speaking of kind hearts, Bertie had pulled some strings for me. I don't know what he said, or if he called in a favor, but Fleischman still didn't bring an accusation against me for hauling The Beef to the freezer or the river—or anywhere for that matter. Holland was pretty frazzled still. He repeated what he saw and did several times. He was released from questioning before I was, but when I came out of the interrogation room, I saw he was still waiting around.

"I'll pop for a cab and a drink," I said. He gladly accepted.

On the ride back to our apartment building he grew more talkative, like someone coming out of shock and seeing life clearly for the first time. I felt guilty that he had to be involved, but took consolation in the possibility that his artistry might benefit. Holland, the struggling artist, who ended the struggle. Go figure. Maybe he'd sculpt wrestling figures after this. I owed him big for saving my life.

We decided to sit in his apartment for our drink. I insisted on bringing over a bottle. By tacit mutual consent, he waited at his place while I went down the hall. I didn't think he'd want to revisit the crime scene so soon. The Super had locked up. Great guy. There was a note on the door not to disturb the room. The note did everything but scream, Crime Scene! You're evicted, asshole! I went in, despite the sign, and aside from the crimson patch on the carpet, everything looked as staid as it usually does. I retrieved the gin bottle, three-quarters full. We'd make a dead soldier of it before the night was through.

I stayed up till about 3:00 A.M. with Holland. He wanted to keep talking, replaying the evening's events until they took on the gloss of a polished keepsake. He would tell this story for the rest of his life. I listened as well as I could, occasionally filling him in on what parts of the case I thought he'd want to hear. He grew chattier with the booze, while I found myself sinking down in my seat. Not easy to do in a rattan chair. Eventually, he was out of gas. It happened suddenly with a big yawn. I told him he'd better sleep. Tomorrow might bring a fresh round of questioning, especially when—or if—Kira regained consciousness.

Going back into my apartment, I stepped over the bloodstain like it was a puppy turd I was too tired to deal with. When this was all over, I'd have to spend a long time contemplating whether I wanted that emblem in blood to figure in my death, too. I think I already knew the answer.

I stripped off my clothes down to a tanktop T-shirt and boxers. The bedroom felt pretty cool, a little moist, but cool. I turned off the window fan and lay under a sheet. Looking up at the ceiling, I waited for unconsciousness to take over. The good kind. The kind brought on by booze, not a choking grip.

I woke up to the phone ringing. It might have been ringing for a while by the time I realized what insistent sound was disturbing my sleep. I picked it up and scratched at my balls.

"Ed? It's Bertie."

I felt relieved and tense at once. "Bertie, what's new?"

"So, I've just heard quite a story. With your name attached to it."

"I win the sweepstakes?" I swallowed dryly. My heart flopped and fluttered.

"Not quite. Attempted murder after forced entry. Happened on my turf, so I got the report."

"I'd be the vic. Attempted, that is. I've already been grilled to a nice golden brown by your friends, by the way." That sounded snide and peremptory. Before I could correct myself, Bertie resumed.

"Well this bright penny detective has got some answering to do. Not only that, he's looking at a subpoena for two, maybe three trials. Coming soon to Market Street."

I restrained myself from cursing. Bertie is so smooth he can guide the conversation from easy banter to gravity, all in the same effortless tone. It works on suspects. Now, he was working it on me.

"All right, Bertie. Who wants to meet me and when?"

"Well, I know I interrupted your beauty rest. It's 10:15 now—you know, some people keep regular hours—how about noon? Start with Dave Fleischman at the Five and you can work your way around the illustrious districts of St. Louis's Finest."

"I've already had the honor. Last evening. And I have to thank—"

"Well, there's more to come, so look sharp and don't be late."

"All right. I'll, uh, I'll be ready." In the pause that followed, I could almost hear the disgusted look forming on his face. I got a sour feeling.

"Ed, that's not all," he began. "Bad news, depending on how you want to look at it."

"Let me guess. Kira?"

"She died this morning. Cardiac arrest."

I looked at my pale, flat feet. "Holland won't take this well."

"No, maybe not. He was saving you, though, don't forget."

"I know." And I saved you, let us remember. "But think of it. He's an artist, not in the life. Such as we call ours."

"True."

For a few seconds we didn't speak. I pulled out a cigarette. "So, now what?"

"Well, Simon and Broad Jimmy are already in custody. Some of my men are interrogating this Ichiro. They'll break him. Not that there's much left to break."

"What's gonna happen to Jimmy?" I more or less knew the answer.

"He's a cop-killer, Ed. Even with your testimony—which, I'm afraid, doesn't add much as far as the judge is concerned—he's gonna go up the ladder fast. If he feels lucky to be alive, he'll sit in a cell in Gumbo till he rots. Whether he feels that way or not, the State of Missouri might decide to make him a deterrent and give him the gas in Jeff City."

"Dammit." I drew on the cigarette. It tasted like a mildewed rag. "Not even his service will be a mitigating factor?"

"I don't care to speculate, Ed. Now, you will be a help against Ichiro and Simon. Problem is, Simon alleges you broke into his house and beat him senseless. If that's true that doesn't help your case out much." He waited on the line, as though his last statement were a question.

"You know how I operate sometimes, Bertie."

He sighed. "Yeah, I do. And I'm not—I can't protect you on that one."

"I know." And I wouldn't ask. I don't think I'll be able to ask again. "What about The Beef?"

"Let's just stick with the known facts. Broad Jimmy hired you to investigate his killing. That's all I've told anyone about." I could imagine something distasteful had crawled up his throat. "Simon was his murderer. You helped uncover that. Maybe the end will justify your means."

"Simon out of the hospital yet?"

"Yeah. He's in a holding cell in District Four. They'll transfer him to our jurisdiction later today."

"Why don't I feel good about any of this?" It was a rhetorical question.

"Something I'd like to know is what Officer Downing was doing at Broad Jimmy's. What he was really doing there."

I considered what to say. "The Beef pissed him off. He was contemplating a little off-the-clock time with him. Not murder—and I'm confident of that. He got tangled up at the wrong time."

"Downing was a good beat cop. Young. No violations of protocol. He's got a wife. Everything was in front of him for the asking."

"Believe me, if there's anything I could have done at that moment—"

"I know that, Ed. Look," he paused again as though prolonging this conversation could only hurt him. "I'm gonna pass you the name and number of that attorney. He's done a helluva job for some of our guys."

"You included?"

Bertie waited. "No. I've never needed him."

That's fair.

"I'm gonna ring off. They're gonna let me walk around outside today. They say it's cooled off. I might even be released in a couple of days. Stay at home or the office. Don't stray from the known numbers, all right?"

"Sure." I didn't bring up the resumption of our card games, or promise to visit again.

"See you later, Ed."

I couldn't bring myself to say anything. He hung up before I had a chance. I ran my fingers through my thinning hair. Sorry, Bertie. Don't cut me out.

I showered and got dressed. I made coffee, again doubling the usual heaping quantity of grounds. I popped some aspirin, too. The combination of strangulation and gin made for a neato headache. My tongue felt like it had spoken its fill, giving voice to the rotten thoughts swirling in my mind.

I pulled into my office in the industrial court around 11:30. The sky was washed of storm clouds and pollution, leaving a beautiful blue with high fans of cirrus. It was cool out, too, just like Bertie had said—maybe in the seventies. I unlocked my office and sat behind the desk. My old chair swayed back on its creaky springs. I put my feet up and lit a smoke. From this vantage point the Bradford Pears outside screened the blue sky, but I could see the street and the preschool. I wondered where Rachel Hanady was and if she'd be back at school anytime soon. What the Feds had discovered, if anything, about the adoption operation in Columbia. How Jerri was doing. I watched the school entrance until my eyes blurred, then rubbed them hard and they cleared.

But no amount of rubbing will clear away the grey in which I live and operate. It covers me. Envelopes me. Keeps me alive—so far, at least. But it can also blind me to the stark black and white, the unadulterated good and evil where they do exist, independent of and resolutely opposing each other. Still, regardless of my failures of discernment, maybe Kira was right about one thing. I do like justice too much.

~ The End. ~

ACKNOWLEDGMENTS

Thanks to Daniel and Julie Smith, for helping Ed first find life in the pages of an experimental story crafted at the University of Iowa School for the Book.

And thanks also to to Pat Horine, for mad dreams at Dressel's Pub Above; Bill and Patty Westphal, for space to write and long encouragement; Scott Phillips and Jedidiah Ayres, who each generously supported my work and jumped me into the world of noir writing; Donna Essner, for her special gift in turning the tables on Ed and making him talk; my mother and father, Mary and Tim Ryan, for pumping *The Third Man* and other film noir greats into my bloodstream at a young age; and my loving wife Dee and daughters Irene and Rosie, without whose support and affection I would be just another lonely man.

ABOUT THE AUTHOR

John Joseph Ryan's short stories have appeared online in Akashic Books' "Mondays are Murder" series, *Shotgun Honey, Out of the Gutter, Suspense Magazine*, and *MARGIN, Exploring Modern Magical Realism*. A verse noir poem appears in Gutter Books' recent anthology *Noir Riot*. His poetry has appeared in various print magazines, including *River Styx* and *Black Buzzard Review*.

John's collaborative story, *Hothouse by the River*, which introduced private detective Ed Darvis, was produced in a limited letter press edition at the University of Iowa School for the Book. He lives in St. Louis with his wife and two children.